MW01227370

WAYWARD
ARROWS

Adrian Chase

Wayward Arrows
A Malaysian MM Romance Novel
Copyright @ 2022 by Adrian Chase
ISBN: 9798839817999
https://www.adrianchase.com

Cover Design by Adrian Chase

This book is a work of fiction. Any references to historical events, real people, or real locales are used fictitiously. Names, characters, places, and incidents are products of the author's imagination, and any resemblance to actual events, locations, or persons, living or dead, is entirely coincidental.

All rights reserved. No part of this book may be reproduced, scanned, or transmitted in any form, digital, audio, or printed, without the expressed written consent of the author.

DEDICATION

To all the boys and girls and those in between who grow up believing their very existence is wrong and defective, I see you.

And to Breanna Teintze, the anchor I've never met, thank you for seeing me.

AUTHOR'S NOTE

Growing up gay in a Muslim-majority country like Malaysia can be permanently damaging. You either repress it and try to grow up "normal" until one day the pressure becomes too much and you explode in a mostly negative manner, or you exist in shadows, ridiculed your entire life if you let slip even a hint of flamboyance. Our deep Southeast Asian heritage complicates things as our lives are deeply entwined with our families'. No matter how old we get, not disappointing our parents and elders is *the* top priority.

I grew up hating myself. It took a massive spiral into Major Depressive Disorder (MDD) and ongoing sessions with a psychiatrist and a psychologist for me to accept that I was not created wrong. I was, and am, precisely who I am supposed to be.

Well, accepting and believing are two different matters. But I'm still learning.

I wasted my youth and young adulthood denying my nature, believing that the things I felt were unnatural. I had no one to turn to, and seeing how poorly effeminate kids my age were treated, I did my best to fit in. I became a master contortionist who forgot his original shape.

I know there are other books I can publish, other stories I can tell that can make better sales, I'm reaching out to kids like my younger self who believe that they are an abomination for liking someone their own gender, for not fitting in their own existence, in hopes that they will not waste their youth contorting themselves.

I hope they find happiness early in their lives.

I hope they love themselves.

PLAYLIST

Name, The Goo Goo Dolls (opening credits)
This Is The Thing, Fink
Wonderwall, Ryan Innes (originally by Oasis)
Freedom! '90, George Michael
How To Save A Life, The Fray
ILYSB - Stripped, Lany
I Can't Make You Love Me, Cinzia & The Eclipse (originally by
Bonnie Raitt)
Ending, Isak Danielson
This Is Me, Keala Settle & The Greatest Showman Ensemble
Make It To Me, Sam Smith (closing credits)

Songs Azraai plays on the guitar:
Always, Francois Klark
Heather, Conan Gray
Dancing On My Own, Callum Scott (originally by Robyn)

1

Sunny days remind me of death. Specifically, they remind me of the day my mom died, and I didn't. It was almost cloudless, just like today, rare for Kuala Lumpur. I can recall so many things about the accident nearly twelve years ago, like the suspended silence before the screech of metal on asphalt overrode all my other senses, or how the windscreen cracked in a million places all at once. I can even recall the sharp stench of petrol and blood. The one thing that remains blank is my mom's face. What's sad is that I can't recognize her even now if someone were to shove her photograph in my face. I lost both my parents that day. But at least I get to visit my mom's grave every Eid or whenever I need to talk to someone. I still share a home with the old man, but we avoid each other like magnets of the same polarity.

Give me rain. I take rainy days anytime.

I cross the football field to get to the student parking lot. The university has this stupid rule of restricting the parking space at the academic block to faculty members only. My shirt is already slurping against my skin as I walk, but this is the fastest route to my car. They provide a roofed pedestrian walkway, but it'll mean an extra ten minutes in this sweltering heat. I don't understand why there are people playing football on the open field, and from the sound of their whoops and laughter, they're enjoying it.

"Watch out!"

I feel the impact before I hear the yell. A football thuds against my left shoulder and ricochets off, sending me staggering for balance. The surprise hits me more than the pain, but my shoulder is already throbbing when I realize what just happened. The guy holding the offending white-and-black football approaches me. The first thing I notice is that he's around my height, which says something; I'm six feet two inches tall. With the sun directly in my line of sight, I'm greeted by a glowing face so bright I have to shield my eyes.

"Whoa, there. Are you all right?"

Strong hands grab my waist as my knees buckle. Even with my eyes closed, the world seems too bright. My ears ring, and my mouth goes dry. This close, I can smell the mixture of sweat and lemon body wash that emanates from him. Not to mention the heat that wafts from his body. I feel even more lightheaded. I hold his forearms for support, but they are slick with sweat.

"Sorry," he says. His voice is deep as the ocean. He doesn't budge until I regain my footing.

"I'm fine," I say, letting go.

"Sure?"

I nod. Big mistake. A fresh wave of nausea hits me. "Just... give me a sec."

"Not going anywhere."

That's when I realize he's still holding my waist. I squirm, and he must have taken it as a signal because he releases his hold but keeps his hands hovering, ready to catch me.

"Is your shoulder all right? Sorry about your shirt."

I blink and glance at my shoulder. My eyes take a moment to focus. A streak of brown mars the white, albeit sweat-drenched fabric. "It's not...?" I ask, taking a whiff.

"Dust and dried mud. I think. Sorry again, ya?"

"Don't sweat it," I say, earning a chuckle. Weird. Few people get my puns.

"If you're sure you're all right, I'll get back to my teammates."

I nod again and wave him away. By the time I focus my eyes enough to take in my surroundings, he has already picked up the ball and is making his way back to the field, his back toward me.

His red jersey displays a large "7", with "JACEN" printed in block capital letters above the number.

When I reach home, the old man's car is already parked on the porch. The hood is still warm. I take a peek inside to make sure the coast is clear before entering.

"Azraai, is that you?" asks Mak Su, the housekeeper, from the kitchen.

My body twitches involuntarily. Mak Su is so loud, she may as well announce my arrival directly to the old man. I make a beeline to the kitchen before she can call out my name the second time, as she usually does whenever I don't answer. The aroma of chicken curry greets me, sending my empty stomach growling.

"Assalamualaikum, Mak Su," I say, giving her a wave as I open the fridge.

"Alaikumsalam. Good, you're in time for dinner. I'm cooking—why is your shirt dirty?"

She rushes to my side and reaches up to inspect my face. I lean forward on instinct. Her full height is at my chest level, but she's the only person who can make me feel like a little boy. Her plump fingers caress the fuzz on my cheeks.

"You didn't get into a fight again, did you?" Mak Su asks, her eyes narrowed. "If anything happens to that handsome face, I'll die from a heart attack."

"You said that the last time," I say, giving her my most charming smile.

"And I mean it every time."

"Where's the old man?"

"In his study. I'm making your favorite dishes. It'll be good to have the two of you at the same table for once."

Nope. Not going to happen. "I promised my friends to work on a project tonight. Keep some in the fridge. I'll eat when I get back."

"Then eat before you leave. I'm almost done, anyway."

I hate to disappoint Mak Su, but what she's asking for is something I cannot deliver. I give her a tight hug. "Really sorry, Mak Su. Next time, maybe."

I duck out before she makes an argument. The rest of the house is quiet, empty despite being filled with furniture and decorations that my mom had hand-picked when my parents moved in here. Well, there have been changes since her death. Paintings and artworks have replaced every single family portrait. This place looks more like an art gallery than a home.

I stop in front of the study on my way to my room. Knowing the old man, the door should be locked. Not that I've tried opening it whenever he's inside for the past ten years or so. I kinda forget what he looks like.

The door clicks and slides open. A weary man with salt-and-pepper hair and beard, both meticulously trimmed, looks at me with surprise written all over his face. He seems smaller than I remember.

"Oh. Azraai. When did you get home?"

I'm not prepared for a conversation, much less a confrontation, as our encounters always go. "Just a pit stop to shower. I'm going out again."

"Oh." The relief in that simple word is palpable.

I turn away and head for my room. Giving him a small wave, I say, "I'm off."

"Okay. You look good, son."

Coming from the old man, it feels like a slap.

2

The Starbucks outlet I frequent is crowded, even though we're living amid a pandemic. Nothing much has changed, except for the requirement to check-in online, body temperature monitoring, and a mandatory face mask upon entry. I already have a black cloth mask on, and I lean forward and push my hair aside so that the barista on duty can point the thermometer at my forehead.

"Hi, Azraai," she says.

"Heyya, June," I say without looking at her tag. Her name is worth memorizing because she remembers my usual orders. But she's extra familiar and chatty with me, which is a minus point.

"Long night here?"

I nod.

"We have a new part-timer. Be gentle, okay?"

I give a half-smile that June cannot see. She knows me too well.

There are plenty of empty tables inside. The night crowd hasn't trickled in, and this is not a place to have dinner. I've always liked the brown-and-gray deco, and the high ceiling makes the cafe spacious. The downside to this is that noise and conversations reverberate everywhere, amplified to a point where it disrupts one's concentration. That's why I often see other kids with laptops and homework come prepared with their hoodies and earphones.

A couple of baristas are tending to drive-through orders, while three others are preparing drinks. One tall Chinese guy in a black uniform and mask is standing at the cashier counter, taking an order from another customer. He must be the new part-timer June mentioned.

I stand behind the yellow line on the floor as I wait for my turn and catch up on Instagram. My last post was three days ago, but it's still getting over two hundred likes and comments that I don't bother reading. I have 310,714 followers... no, two more people just followed me. The hundred or so people that I actually know are lost among the throng of strangers. I can post a blurred photo of myself and still garner at least twenty thousand likes.

I'm looking at a model friend's holiday post at Tioman Island when the barista gives a cheerful "Hi, welcome to Starbucks!"

I cannot possibly leave such a spirited greeting unrewarded. Sorry, June. "I'd like a venti vanilla latte, with an extra shot. The coffee, not vanilla. Iced, but not too much, sugar-free, with low-fat milk."

He raises an eyebrow as he writes on the transparent cup. "Okay. Do you want any food to go with the drink?"

"Wait. You got everything?"

He repeats my order, but honestly, I've forgotten the exact details of the drink I asked for. I don't even know if it'll taste good. But it sounds about right. Impressive.

"June said you're new."

He gives a low chuckle. "Yeah, they're understaffed here, so management transferred me from the Great Eastern Mall branch. So you want any food?"

"I'll have chicken lasagna with extra cheese."

"Good choice. Can I get your name, please?"

"Azraai," I say, but I don't spell it out for him.

"You look familiar, by the way. Have we met before?"

I've been told that I have soulful eyes, whatever that means, but I doubt anyone can recognize me based on my eyes alone. Sure, the barista has double-lidded eyelids that are not common among the Chinese community, and thick, symmetrical brows, but with the rest of his face hidden behind the mask, there's no way I can tell who he is.

"Do you read fashion magazines?" I ask.

"Should I?"

"Do you follow my I-G account?"

"Should I?"

I scoff and wave my card at the infrared reader to pay for my dinner. "Then we don't know each other," I say.

"Have a seat. I'll send your food and drink once they're ready."

I pick an empty spot with a wall power socket under the square two-seater desk near the rear exit, which is now inaccessible. I take off my mask and continue browsing through my social media feeds.

"How's your shoulder?"

I absently rub my left shoulder without looking up. "Fine. Doesn't hurt." Then, realizing what's happening, I whip around to see the barista standing behind me, holding a brown tray with both hands.

"I knew you looked familiar," he says. I can tell that he's smiling from the way his mask shifts. "Sorry again about the football thing."

"Jacen?"

"You know my name?"

I make vague pointing gestures at my back.

"My jersey. Got it. Here's your food," he says, setting the tray on my desk.

I take the cup and inspect his handwriting. "Huh. You *almost* got my name right."

"I did?"

"It's A-Z-R-A-A-I, with a double A, not A-Z-R-A-I. But close enough."

"Got it. Well, enjoy your meal."

"Thanks," I say, but he's already walking away. He has broad shoulders and a tapered waist. Soon enough, I lose interest as I try to figure out a way to kill five hours before I have to return home. I take a sip, stop, look at the cup, and then take another sip.

I guess I have a new favorite drink. If I can remember what exactly I ordered, that is.

As expected, the night crowd is obnoxiously loud. Even with my earphones on and the music volume is almost at full blast, the cacophony still thumps against my eardrums like an army of Dothraki on a rampage.

I've been reading *Starting a Business for Dummies* for the past two hours because one of my course's electives is on startup businesses, and the textbook is too dry. But even with this dumbed-down version, there's only so much I can take in one sitting. I stretch my neck and let my eyes linger a little longer than necessary on this one guy across from me. He's sitting with five other guys, and they're talking about some useless shit like the English Premier League or something, as if they're professional sports commentators and the entire cafe is their audience. I notice he keeps stealing glances at me for the past hour. His looks are passable, a bit older than me, maybe, and he's fair-skinned for a Malay, though nowhere near my skin tone. He keeps positioning himself to best show off his muscular arms and pecs straining under his dark blue collared T.

Leaving my book on the desk beside two empty cups, I stretch further and head for the restroom. They built the male toilet for one occupant, but I leave the door unlocked. I freshen up and wait for a few minutes, but no one even attempts to turn the doorknob. Maybe I read the signals wrong.

Disappointed, I open the door only to discover the guy standing outside, fidgeting. He's almost a head shorter, but he definitely has the bulk. "You don't do this often, huh?" I ask, my voice as low as possible, it's almost a purr. "Let me make this easy on you. I'm going to walk slowly to my car. If no one follows me, I'll go home."

The guy still looks lost, so I squeeze between him and the doorway to retrieve my book and leave the cafe. I parked a little way down the road, at an empty parking lot where the orange streetlight flickers, a perfect setup for a slasher movie.

I hear the shuffle of footsteps behind me, but I don't turn to look. This can go either way: the guy has gathered his nerves to follow me, or he has taken offense at my suggestion and the entire group is going to beat me up. I don't care.

I sit behind the steering wheel and start the engine before pushing back the seat. The guy stands outside the passenger's side, waiting for an invitation. I sigh and open the door. He's really new to this. It's almost annoying if I wasn't so horny.

He takes a seat, eases the door closed, and stares at me. Sweat beads trickle down his temples. "You look better in person," he says. He has a surprisingly pleasant voice, but we're not here to start a conversation.

"So you follow my I-G."

"Can I… can I kiss you?"

"Not on the lips."

His movements are hesitant and awkward, partly because of the cramped space. He kisses my cheek and jaw and neck and Adam's apple. When he aims for my earlobe, I twist away. There's nothing more annoying than the amplified sounds of someone slobbering. He feels me under my T-shirt and plays with my nipples.

Okay. Maybe he's not *that* new to this, after all.

By the time he unzips my jeans, I'm already hard. He takes me in his mouth, and I let out a soft gasp. He stops long enough to look at me and ask, "Can I jerk off here?"

I shrug. "Do whatever you want."

He slips his sweatpants and boxers down to mid-thigh and plays with himself. I barely give him any attention. Instead, I guide his greasy head deeper until he gags. In less than a minute, he lets go of me and explodes on the dashboard and windscreen. Quite impressive, really.

"I'm... sorry. Sorry for the mess! Do you have tissue paper?"

"Don't bother," I say as I tuck my dick back into my shorties and zip up my jeans.

"But you're not done yet."

Understatement of the year. This is annoying. *He's* annoying.

"So? You obviously are," I say.

I nod at the door, and he takes it as a cue that our time is over. He glances at me, then at the goo that's starting to drip off the windscreen, and then back at me. He slips his pants back on and exits the car.

One thing I've learned to prevent other people from bragging about what they do with me is to leave them wondering where they did wrong. Once the confusion settles, the guilt that follows will do the rest.

When I glance at the rearview mirror, the guy is still standing under the flickering light, staring into the dark nothingness.

3

The thing about a business degree course in a private university is that at least half the class comprises children of business tycoons, and most of them don't really want to be here. The heirs of wealthier and more influential magnates are sent overseas, though I doubt they prefer studying over living their best social lives there, either. I still wonder why I declined the offer to study in Melbourne when it meant getting the hell away from home.

Even though I am the only heir of an influential business magnate, I have no intention of walking in the old man's footsteps. I just happen to like business.

Vidya, one of the few people I tolerate, is an heir to a throne, too, albeit a lesser one. We also share the same modeling agency, although calling the lazy opportunists an agency is giving them too much credit. But unlike me, she's following this course under duress. She takes none of the classes seriously. It's enough that she attends them.

What's worse is that she makes a conscious effort to disrupt my concentration during classes. I have no idea why I tolerate her company.

"Babe, they asked me to ask you if you could model for the uni's print ad," she whispers, leaning close. Here I thought alternate seating in the lecture hall as part of social distancing would afford me more personal space, but Vidya doesn't see it as a deterrent.

"Why don't you do it?" I whisper back. And why wouldn't she? Part Indian, part French, she turns heads wherever she goes. People even call us the power couple of the university, but she likes girls as much as I like guys. It's amusing how people choose to see what they want to block off what they cannot accept.

"They want the two best-looking freshie boys to be the talents. You're the most gorgeous guy in this entire shit hole, so I don't understand this freshie business."

"Who's the other one?"

"Someone from mass com. I have no idea who he is, though."

"Who's 'they'? The ones who asked you to ask me," I say.

"Your fan club."

"My *what*?"

Vidya rolls her eyes and hands me her phone. There's a WhatsApp group called 'AzraAiNi'. "Ai ni is —"

"Love you. Yeah, Vid. I speak Mandarin, duh. But what…." I scroll through the chat history and find candid shots of me, voyeuristic video clips of me eating or walking or just standing there doing my own thing, and announcements that I'm their future husband. I give a choking snort, which earns the lecturer's attention. Not knowing what else to do, I raise my hand in apology, and she resumes imparting her wisdom to the whiteboard. Now it's my turn to lean toward Vidya. "You know they don't stand a chance in hell, right?"

"Oh, there are boys in the group, too."

I can't decide if I'm flattered or creeped out. I narrow my eyes. "Why are you in it?"

Vidya snatches her phone and gives me a grin that displays her perfect teeth. She maintains that they're all-natural, but I have my suspicions. "Because it's fun. Because classes are a bore, and I want to be entertained. So are you in or not?"

"No."

She plays with her carefully curated curls. "Aren't you the least bit curious about who this other handsome person is?"

Well, she got me there.

Vidya takes my resigned sigh as a yes. She bites her lower lip as she types on her phone. I notice that some of the boys are staring at her. I'm sure she sees them, too. "Oh. They also want you to bring your guitar," she says.

"How do they even know I play the guitar?"

Vidya rolls her eyes again as if I'm the densest person she has come across. "Babe, who do you think follow your Insta?"

Again, she got me there.

I've never been to the Schools of Arts block, and I must admit, it's much livelier than our drab business block. More colorful, too, with paintings and photographs on the walls, and even a floor-to-ceiling mural at the staircase. Almost half the lobby space is taken up by a maze-like formation of blue soft boards adorned with a mixture of traditional and 3D cartoon illustrations. The School of Graphics must be having a showcase or something.

On one of the granite benches in the common area, two girls are playing the guitar. It's like they're challenging each other in a friendly competition. They have a small audience built up, appreciating the song they're playing. "Closer", by The Chainsmokers. Both of them have some serious skills. I tug at my Epiphone's case strap, itching to join them. But I don't think they'll welcome the intrusion, and I'll be late if I get distracted any further.

The high-ceilinged hall doubles as a photo studio, and as studios go, this one is fully decked. Not like some of the 'professional' studios I've had photoshoots in. They've set the far end of the hall up with a floor-to-wall white backdrop with a black high stool in the middle. Strobe lights and reflector screens surround the stool in an arc, and one guy is adjusting the camera on a tripod, while the other is checking the test shots on his laptop. The third guy and one girl are playing with their phones at the makeup and costumes station by the side. The racks are empty, and so are the vanity counters, but I can imagine how chaotic things can get if the School of Fashion occupies this space.

I clear my throat. "I'm here for the print ad shoot. Thanks for waiting." They may be my age and fellow students, not professional photographers, but I'm a professional model. Being courteous goes a long way.

The guy fiddling with the camera looks up and rushes to greet me. He offers his hand for me to shake but retracts it in an awkward motion. I guess all of us are still adjusting to the new norm. "Azraai? Wow, you look way better in person. Sorry for postponing the shoot. The other talent had a quiz and we're only allowed to use this place for one session."

"No worries. Thanks for having me."

"I hope there wasn't an issue with your agent?"

"I told him this is a pro-bono student project. He's not happy someone other than him gets to exploit me, but my contract is…loose. So don't worry about it," I say, followed by a soft chuckle. "Who's the other talent, anyway?"

"I don't know if you know him. Quan Zhen Xin, from Mass Communication. Star athlete. He was here, but he went out to borrow a basketball."

I don't know what concept they have in mind, and how a guitar and a basketball are relevant in promoting the university, but I ask nothing. My approach is to let the art director take the lead, and I do my best to fulfill their vision. I only ask questions when I need some clarification.

I learned this the hard way.

The boy and girl who were occupied with their phones direct me to one of the makeup counters. They're both giggling as they attend to me. I'm not sure which of them is more excited to be this close to me, but I find their colorful masks more interesting than the faces partially hidden behind them. At least the girl is brave enough to ask for a selfie with me. I wonder if the photo will end up in that crazy WhatsApp group.

She's applying foundation on my forehead when the door shuffles open, and in walks a guy who towers over the rest. He's wearing a blue-and-white sleeveless jersey that fully displays his lean but muscular shoulders and arms, and a pair of skinny jeans that fits him perfectly. He's not wearing a mask. As he walks closer, I get to see his face more clearly. Strong eyebrows, a sharp nose, full lips, and square, clean-shaven jaws. I can cut paper with that jawline. What strikes me the most is how symmetrical his features are. He doesn't have that international look as I do, but he can definitely give me a run for my money.

Note to self: thank Vidya for talking me into doing this gig.

I play it cool by concentrating on getting my makeup done, if you'd call a layer of foundation and some lip balm that. I'm having doubts about this production. The small guy who was extra excited to greet me leads the much taller talent to the vanity next to mine. I nod to acknowledge his presence.

"We meet again, Azraai with a double A," he says, giving me a left-sided smile.

Wait. I study his face closer. Double eyelids, symmetrical eyebrows. "Jacen?"

He gives a laugh that fills the entire studio. Everyone turns to look at him. "Ouch. Didn't know I was that forgettable."

As if anyone can ever forget a face like his. "I was out of whack after you hit me with the ball. And you had that mask on at Starbucks."

13

"Got it," he says, still chuckling.

"The photographer said your name was Quan... something."

"Zhen Xin. Yeah, that's my official name. Everyone except my parents calls me Jacen."

"What do they call you?"

"Ah Boy."

Before I can talk further, the small guy stands between us to apply foundation on Jacen's face. I can see Jacen's reflection stiffening.

"First time getting makeup on your face?" I ask.

Jacen attempts to nod, but the small guy holds his chin in place. Jacen jerks away at the physical contact and then mumbles an apology. He allows the guy to hold his face, but his tense posture and the fair knuckles that grip the chair betray his discomfiture.

"Relax, it's just foundation. He hasn't even applied eyeshadow and lipstick," I say, quickly losing interest. I don't pursue straight guys. They're generally a mess, and it's not an experience I intend to repeat ever again.

Jacen jerks away again to look at me, his eyes wide. I give half a smile and leave him with his tormentor, who's complaining for Jacen to keep still. I saunter to the photographer with the guitar case in my hand. Letting go of the camera, he looks up at me and smiles.

"Good, you're ready," he says.

"How do you want to do this?"

"Meaning?"

My instinct was on point. Note to self: forget gratitude. I'm going to kill Vidya. I sigh inwardly to tune down my annoyance. "What's your direction for this shoot? Casual? Professional? High fashion?"

The photographer gives me a sheepish smile. "To be honest, I'm more into landscape and still life. My senior is sick, so I'm filling in for him. You're a model, right? Can you lead the shoot?"

I stretch my neck and then take a seat on the stool surrounded by strobes. "Tell me what this is for, and we'll go from there."

"It's for the extracurricular clubs' registration day. We want to promote the event, and the seniors think your face on the fliers and posters will boost attendance."

I unzip the guitar case and take out the Epiphone. Its dark brown vignette surface gives a pleasing contrast to my fair complexion under the glare of white light. At least the assistant has enough sense to carry the case away. I sandwich the Epiphone between my lap and elbow. When the photographer doesn't budge, I point my chin at the camera on the tripod. He gives me another apologetic smile before rushing to bury his face behind the DSLR. I give several casual poses as the camera clicks at a frantic pace. Then I stand up with the Epiphone in front of me, my hands holding the headstock. I show off with a bit of high fashion, which earns squeals from the makeup crew.

When the photographer gives me a thumbs-up signal, I'm already starting to sweat. I nod back and store the Epiphone in its case. As I approach the photographer, I sling it across my shoulders. "That's it, right? We're done for the day?"

"Yes. Thank you so much for doing this. All your photos look so good. We're going to have a tough time choosing." He then hands me a white envelope.

They have promised me two hundred ringgit for the shoot, but what my agent doesn't know won't cause any problems. I usually carry more cash than this in my wallet, but a professional never declines monetary payment.

I'm about to leave when I hear the photographer failing miserably at attempting to direct Jacen. With my hand still on the doorknob, I turn to watch Jacen standing in the middle of the stage with the basketball firmly in his grasp, looking like a burglar caught in a police helicopter spotlight.

This is going to be entertaining.

I rest the Epiphone against the wall and continue watching in silence. Soon enough, the photographer raises both hands in frustration, and the assistant starts to coach Jacen. The best part is that none of them seem to know what they're doing. Jacen knots his eyebrows and tries his best to mimic the assistant's poses, but each move is more cringe-worthy than the previous one.

When it gets too painful to watch, I step in. All of them look surprised that I'm still around, but the photographer's expression quickly turns into a desperate plea for help.

"Don't tell me it's your first time in front of the camera," I say. I fold my sleeves and push my hair back. This is going to take more effort than the two hundred ringgits' worth.

"Not like this," Jacen says, gesturing at the strobes. He is covered in sweat.

"Go freshen up and let them repair your face. You're a mess."

When Jacen returns from the toilet, he's just as tense as before. He grips the basketball like a lifeline. His jersey is drenched, whether from tap water or sweat, I don't know.

"Did you bring spare clothes?" I ask.

"I have a clean T-shirt in my bag."

"Go change."

I sit at the makeup counter while I wait. The small guy must think that he's being surreptitious at taking a photo of me using his phone, but I don't think he notices his reflection in the vanity mirror. I glance away. That's when I see Jacen's back reflected in the other mirror as he changes out of the jersey. His smooth back spreads like a map I wouldn't mind exploring, and the defined muscles ripple with each movement. A deep line cuts a trench along the middle, down his narrow waist, and disappears under the gray underwear band that peeks out of his jeans.

I quickly look away when he puts on a black T-shirt, and then pretend to notice his reflection for the first time when he turns, fully clothed. "Done? Come. Sit," I say, pointing at the empty chair beside me.

A gamut of expressions shifts across his face as he watches me take the compact powder from the makeup box. He's about to say something but stops himself.

I dab the round pad on the powder foundation before giving his face my full attention. He is beautiful, for someone who obviously has no clue about facial care other than a thorough shave. "Keep still. I've never done this on anyone other than myself."

Jacen raises an eyebrow but says nothing. Neither does he move as I apply the foundation. I can smell his lemon body wash. I'm not surprised if he uses the same soap to clean his face. Once I'm done with the powder, I use my pinkie to run some balm over his perfectly pink lips, which he instinctively parts. He has soft lips.

"Done. Go take your place under the light. I'll follow you in a bit," I say. I force myself to think about dogs getting cooked to kill my hard-on.

"Got it. Give me a minute." After a few awkward seconds, he swivels up, straightens his T-shirt, and walks away.

Once I'm confident I won't embarrass myself, I get up and follow him to where the others are waiting. I bounce the basketball on the floor before tossing it to Jacen. He catches it with casual ease.

"Nice pass," he says.

"Nice catch."

I stand beside the photographer and instruct Jacen to stand a little farther back, where the lights can land on him without creating harsh shadows. He still looks unsure, but when I tell him to strike a pose, he becomes totally lost. I walk up to him until we're just a breath apart. He doesn't budge, but his grip on the ball tightens, as though to stop me from coming any closer. We stand at almost the same height. I look at him directly in the eyes, daring him to look away first.

"What are you doing?" he whispers.

"Concentrate on me. Nothing else exists. Not the camera, not the crew, not the studio. Smile. Not like that. Don't force it. Imagine you're at Starbucks, greeting a customer. That's it. Just like that."

I hold Jacen's arms. A jolt of static prickles our skin. He gives a little jump but doesn't move away. I guide his body like a sculptor working with clay. He keeps his eyes on me, as if daring *me* to look away first. I take that as a challenge. I put my hands on his waist, twist it a little, and then use my foot to part his legs, all the while not shifting my gaze.

"Good. Stay like this. Remember, nothing else exists," I say.

I take my place behind the photographer, and he snaps away. I show several more poses for Jacen to mimic, and this time, he does it reasonably well. He even balances the spinning ball on his forefinger while looking at me. Okay, now he's just showing off.

"Try giving them a taste of high fashion," I say.

"How?"

"Stop smiling. Show me your serious face. Tilt your chin up a little. Yes, like that. Try to look as if you're better than everyone else here."

"Better than you?"

"I'm the lowest scum. I'm an ikan bandaraya."

That earns me a laugh that fills the entire studio again. I can't help but smile at him, and he smiles back, wider.

The photographer has to clear his throat to get my attention. "Azraai, since you're here, can I get a couple of shots of you together? Saves the trouble of having to edit and superimpose you in later."

"Sure," I say. I fetch my Epiphone and return to stand beside Jacen. I prop the guitar up before me, and Jacen rests the basketball against his hip. Just as we're about to finalize the pose, he places his right arm on my shoulder. I turn my head to look at him, and he looks right back at me.

We end up doing more than a couple of shots, more than what I get paid for, anyway. We take turns sitting on the stool. Jacen still needs my direction for almost every pose, but by the end of the shoot, he has relaxed enough to look natural in front of the camera.

When we're finally done, it's already almost five. I walk out first while Jacen is getting paid, but as I press the 'down' elevator button, he jogs toward me, gym bag and basketball precariously balanced in his hands.

"Wait up," he says as I step into the elevator.

Once we're in, Jacen clamps the basketball between his knees and slings the bag across his shoulder. "Man, you walk fast," he says.

"Long legs."

He chuckles as he retrieves the ball. "Hey, thanks for rescuing me back there."

"I wouldn't call that a rescue."

"It was a disaster before you stepped in. *I* was a disaster."

"That is true," I say with a solemn nod.

Jacen holds up his white envelope like it were a lifetime achievement award. "What will you do with your money?"

"I don't know. Petrol. Dinner. Maybe both. You?"

While he contemplates an answer, the elevator dings, and the doors slide open. I walk out without waiting, and Jacen has to hasten his steps to catch up to me.

Before he can say anything, a group of six guys hanging out at a concrete bench notice me and start whistling and catcalling. I ignore their jeers and leers and walk straight ahead. While I'm used to this, I prefer it not to be witnessed by somebody I barely know. I only stop outside the building when Jacen grabs my arm.

"Hey. What was that about?"

"Stupid boys being stupid."

"I don't get it. You're bigger than all of them. And you look like you can take them on without breaking a sweat."

I shrug. Jacen lets go.

I'm nowhere near effeminate. While under normal circumstances I'd be inclined to agree with Jacen, what I don't tell him is that the guy who started the catcall had walked in on me and another boy exiting a toilet stall a few weeks ago. It was one of the basement bathrooms on the main block that no one went to. Or so I thought.

"Just ignore the boys," he says.

"What boys?" I ask, giving him the brightest smile that I don't mean.

"Got it. Hey, I know what I'll do with this money. I'm going to pay you for your help with food."

"You're going to give me a free drink and donut at Starbucks?"

Jacen grins at me. Only his smile is genuine. "No, not Starbucks. An actual meal. You pick the place, and I'll pay. But not today. I'm going to be late for work as it is."

"What do you want to eat?"

"I don't know. Anything." The hallmark and bane of all Malaysians.

"You're going to regret saying that."

"Anything within two hundred ringgit, then."

Jacen rushes off to the motorcycle parking outside the building after saying goodbye. I cross the field to get to my car. Gray clouds have blotted out most of the sky, so the temperature is bearable. It starts to drizzle just as I reach my car, bringing with it the fresh scents of grass and hot asphalt. My kind of weather.

I'm already out of the campus when the rain pours in earnest. I wonder if Jacen is caught in the rain. And then I realize that he and I didn't exchange phone numbers.

So much for that free meal.

4

It takes less than three days after the shoot for our faces to be posted all over the campus. I'm used to seeing myself in magazine spreads and billboards, so seeing the posters and fliers everywhere doesn't faze me. I wonder how Jacen is taking it.

The one thing that I find annoying is that other students and some staff members now openly request selfies with me. Vidya makes things worse by offering to help take the photos whenever she's around. If she charges them for the service, then at least I'll know she hasn't been completely wasting her time in business school.

Vidya finds these random impromptu photoshoots hilarious. She directs the girls to stand closer to me or for me to bend my knees so that the height difference won't be too bad. Whenever I decline a selfie request, Vidya will act all dramatic to force me into submission. Before long, the girls learn to only ask for a selfie whenever Vidya is with me, which is almost always.

What's worse is that they tag me in their posts, flooding me with notifications. This morning alone, I've gained sixty-eight new followers and countless DMs that I never intend to read.

Vidya and I are having lunch at the main block's cafe when I notice a girl peeling off one of the promo posters from the wall and then running away with it. "Did you see that?" I ask Vidya.

She follows my gaze at the now bare portion of the wall. "What, that? It's been happening everywhere. I heard they had to keep reprinting new ones to replace the stolen posters. I have one, too."

"You... why?"

"You didn't tell me how hot Jacen was."

"Because he's not your type."

Vidya tilts her head toward me and gives a sly smile. Her nose ring glitters in the fluorescent light. "Babe, he's *everyone's* type. Just because I don't want to ride him doesn't mean I can't appreciate such eye candy."

"What about me?"

"No offense, babe. I love you, but you're an acquired taste. You're also competition."

Whenever I shave, my face gains this androgynous look. I've even done makeup commercials. That's why I keep my facial hair unless a job specifically requires me to get rid of it.

Two girls in plain hijabs approach our desk. One of them keeps nudging the other forward. Vidya particularly likes girls in hijab, so she pays them more attention than I do. I stab at what's left of my lunch, already expecting how this scene will unfold.

"Hi, Azraai. Vidya. We were wondering… umm…" says the girl who's been nudged toward me.

"So cute. Come, give me your phone. Azraai doesn't mind," Vidya says. She offers her meticulously manicured hand.

The girl does as she's told, and the two hijabis flank me as I shoot lasers at Vidya with my eyes.

"Smile," Vidya says, and snaps. "Sorry, that was the front-facing camera. Let's try this again. Smile."

And that is how Vidya inserts herself in the photo library of girls she fancies.

Just as she returns the phone, it dings. So does Vidya's. And the other girl's. And at least half the phones in the cafe. Soon, a barrage of pinging sounds fills the entire place. Only mine remains quiet.

Vidya checks her phone and laughs. "Oh, this is…. Babe, check these out."

My phone chirps from Vidya's incoming message. She's forwarded me a photo of me sitting in front of the vanity counter in the studio. I knew it. The small guy must be in the stupid WhatsApp group, too.

"So what? This is nothing to be excited about," I say.

All around me, people are buzzing and stealing glances at me. Even the two girls are blushing and squealing as they retreat. It's making me uncomfortable, which is rare.

"Wait. Sending you more. The Wi-Fi here is horrendous," Vidya says.

My phone chirps in rapid succession. I see photos of me holding Jacen's shoulders, and then his waist, and other pictures of us together that didn't make the cut. They look... intimate.

"Your fans have mixed reactions over these photos," Vidya says, her face still buried in her phone. "They're disappointed they won't get to be your wife, but at the same time, they're trying to come up with a hashtag to ship the two of you. #JaceAz?"

"Sounds like Jesus."

"You're right. Pass. #AzCen?"

"Ascend?"

Vidya gives an exasperated huff. "Oh, for Christ's sake. Are they shipping you or are they starting a religious cult? #JaceRaai sounds decent, but surely there's something better. Help me out a bit here."

"Why?" I ask.

"What's his name?"

"Jacen."

Vidya kicks my shin real good. It hurts. "Not that name. His Chinese name."

"Why'd you have to kick me, Vid? It's Quan Zhen Xin. Ow."

Vidya puckers her lips, ignoring my pain. "What about #QuanAz? Almost sounds like panas. That's Malay for hot, right?"

I hesitate before answering. I am so going to regret this. "Yes?"

Vidya squeals, and then bites her lower lip. "Ooh, I like that. And you keep telling me my Malay sucks. I am so submitting that hashtag. Look, it's getting upvoted. By a lot."

"You're... you're voting?"

"Why not? You'd make a *hot* couple. Someone even said the two of you are so QuanAz, they need to call 994."

I knock on the desk to vie for Vidya's attention. "Vid, look at me. He's as straight as they come. It's never going to happen. No one needs to call the firefighters. Kill the hashtag, please."

"Are you sure? Even after seeing this?"

My phone chirps again. I'm finding the sound as annoying as Vidya. The photo she forwarded me is of me and Jacen standing side by side, with his arm casually folded on my shoulder, and we turned our heads toward each other. I looked surprised, but he was beaming.

In a different world, maybe this photo would mean something. But we're in *this* world. *This* reality. I tap the side button to put the phone in sleep mode.

In *this* world, my reflection, alone, stares back at me.

* * *

My trepidation about coming home lifts when I see the empty driveway. I call out for Mak Su loudly, expecting her to be in the kitchen preparing dinner. When she doesn't answer, I poke my head into the kitchen to find it empty. Just as I reach the top floor landing, I see her exiting my room with a laundry basket in her hands.

Mak Su's face lights up when she sees me. "Azraai. I didn't hear you come in. Did you say 'assalamualaikum'?"

"Yes, Mak Su."

"Good boy. Alaikumsalam."

"You didn't have to clean my room. But thanks, anyway."

She lifts the overflowing basket higher. "I was wondering why you didn't have any dirty clothes to wash. At this rate, you'll have nothing left to wear by next week."

"Sorry, Mak Su. You didn't... find anything, did you?"

She stops smiling and narrows her eyes. Her face turns all business. "Was I *not* supposed to find anything there, Azraai Yusoff?" She only uses my full name whenever I piss her off or when she thinks she's on to me.

"No," I mumble. Then, hoping to change the subject, I say, "What's for dinner?"

"I thought you didn't want to eat the food I cook anymore?"

"Who gave you that idea?"

"I was thinking of making Chinese steamed sea bass, but maybe I'll just heat all the dishes in the fridge that you promised to eat but didn't."

I scratch the back of my head. I need a haircut; I can bury my hand in my curls. "You can feed me moldy food and I'll still finish the whole plate, Mak Su."

She puts the laundry basket on the floor and reaches up to pat my face. I lean down to let her. Then she whacks my arm. "Such a sweet talker. Your charm may work on girls, but not on me. Now help me carry this basket downstairs. My back hurts."

When I return to my room, I find that Mak Su has done more than pick up my laundry. The entire room has been transformed. She cleans my room at least twice a month, but never on a fixed schedule. I make my bed, but not to her level of military-grade crispness. She has changed the sheets to the set with green, white, and brown leaf motifs, and the Epiphone is on its stand instead of on the bed. The heavy curtains have been changed to complement the sheets and drawn back to let the evening light in. Even my laptop and gaming rigs are organized once more. The carpeted floor is free from discarded clothes. I also know there will be fresh towels in my adjoining bathroom.

The only thing I'm interested in is my underwear drawer. I keep my undies organized so that Mak Su won't be inclined to do it for me. At the back of the drawer is my stash of condoms, and at the bottom is a folder where I keep all my test results. Once I'm certain they have not been discovered, I let out a relieved sigh. Locking the drawer would have only raised suspicion, and my tactic has worked well so far.

Mak Su will surely have a heart attack for real if she discovers what I really am. I don't even want to think what the old man would do.

Mak Su calls me down for dinner just as I get out of the shower. I quickly get dressed in my gym tank top and knee-length shorts. On my way to the kitchen, I check the porch. The old man is not back yet.

Mak Su has set the table for two. There's an actual dining hall with a fancy table that sits twelve, but we usually have dinner together at a much smaller table in the kitchen. My plate is already filled with steaming white rice, but the other plate still lies face-down. Mak Su has prepared turmeric stir-fry chicken, omelet with shrimp and onion, and broccoli with oyster sauce. She's a fantastic cook, but I love these simple dishes the most. I take out a jug of chilled water from the fridge before taking my seat.

"Let's eat, Mak Su."

"You go ahead. You must be famished," she says. She then sits across from me, but not where the plate has been set.

"Is something wrong?"

"No, no. I just want to see you eat. You've been coming home so late this past week."

"Sorry, Mak Su. Been busy with assignments," I say, which is true.

I'm about to take my third handful of rice when the old man enters the kitchen and sits in front of the other table setting. I look at Mak Su, but she doesn't quite meet my eyes. She must have planned this trap.

I stand up and lift my plate even though it's still full. I've suddenly lost my appetite.

"Azraai, please, sit down. It's difficult enough to get the two of you under the same roof at the same time. Your father has something to say. Please," Mak Su says. Concern is written all over her face.

She's the only reason I return to my seat. "But the car?"

"Razali took it for an overnight service," says the old man.

I resent the trap they sprung on me, but for him to rope in the one person in the world that he knows I trust, he must have something terribly important to say. Maybe he's dying. Or he wants to kick me out, finally. Or he wants me to return the credit card. And car.

"You know this Thursday is your mother's death anniversary," he says.

Actually, I didn't know that. I don't even remember her birthday.

"I've always organized a tahlil and dinner for the congregation under your name at the mosque every year, but since it's not workable this year…" he says, trailing off.

Mosques and other houses of worship have been allowed to hold congregations again for the past two months but under strict protocols. Even the way the congregation prays is now different, standing an arm's length apart instead of shoulder to shoulder. I don't pray, but I'm not completely ignorant, either.

"So do it next year," I say.

"I was hoping you'd know any charity or orphanages that we can donate to instead."

"Surely your company has a network of charities for your tax exemption. Sorry, *donations*."

"I want this to be something the two of us can do together," he says.

"Why?"

"Look, son. I'm trying here." He reaches out to hold my hand, but I pull away.

"Trying to do what, exactly? It's a little too late to pretend to be a dad, don't you think?"

"Azraai—" Mak Su starts, but I cut her off.

"Don't say anything, Mak Su."

My low voice must have come out as a warning because she clamps her mouth shut. The old man slumps in his seat. He looks older, smaller. Diminished.

Before anyone can say anything, I surge up and leave them. I don't even bother to wash my hands. Rice still sticks to my right hand when I retrieve my set of keys and storm out of the house.

5

I drove with no destination in mind, as long as it was far from home. I don't know how I ended up in the parking lot near Starbucks. Maybe because I come here so often at night, my body acted on reflex. I'm not dressed to be out in public, but being alone with my thoughts in the car right now makes me claustrophobic. Fuck the old man. And fuck him for roping Mak Su into betraying my trust.

It's drizzling, and by the time I reach the cafe, my bare arms are dotted with beads of raindrops. I expect it to be cold inside, but the seats on the porch are all taken.

A barista stops me just as I'm about to open the door. "Sir? You need to register and get your temperature checked first, sir," he says.

I'd forgotten about it. "Sorry. I left my phone and mask at home."

He hands me a clipboard and a pen. "It's okay. Just write your name and phone number here. Can you lean forward a bit, please? I need to check your temperature."

Once inside, I wait in line to place my order. I barely register my surroundings; the exchange with the old man and Mak Su's betrayal crowd my headspace. When I reach the counter, I absently say, "The usual."

The barista stares back at me with her eyebrows raised.

"Sorry, it's—"

"Venti iced Americano, double shot. Less ice. Mushroom soup with jumbo croissant and butter."

I whip around to see Jacen standing behind me, with a black rectangle bucket filled with dirty plates and cutleries in his hands. His mask moves upward when he smiles.

"Oh, and it's Azraai, with a double A," he adds.

"Thanks," I say after a dumbfounded pause. "How did you know?"

"June told me." He then walks away and disappears behind the swinging door beside the food display counter.

I pay for my meal with the money I found in the white envelope I left on the passenger seat, and then pick a seat at the farthest corner. It's still as noisy as the rest of the place, but at least it's nowhere near any air-conditioning outlets. By the time my food arrives, though, I'm already sitting on the back of my hands and gently rocking back and forth to generate body heat.

"Are you okay?" Jacen asks as he places my food on the table.

"This doesn't concern you," I snap.

"Okay, got it. Enjoy your meal."

"Sorry. That was uncalled for. Things are a little messed up," I say before Jacen turns away.

"My bad. I didn't mean to pry. I thought you were just cold."

"I am. Didn't plan on going out tonight. I didn't even bring my wallet and phone. Is the air-conditioning here always this cold?"

Jacen leans closer and mock-whispers, "Stops the customers from getting too comfortable. Some of them buy one tall drink and stay here for hours."

I blurt out a chuckle despite myself. "Hey. I do that sometimes."

"Yes, and we appreciate it if you buy a drink for every hour you spend here," he says without missing a beat. "Wait here."

"Not going anywhere."

I play with the soup, hungry but with no appetite to eat. When Jacen returns, he offers me a brown leather jacket.

"What's this?"

"You're obviously cold, and there's someplace you don't want to be. You can borrow my jacket, but I need it back," he says.

I can't read his face, partly because of the black mask. "Do you treat all your customers this well or do you want your face to be on that employee of the month board?"

"Seeing my face all over campus is already more than I can handle. I don't know how you do it. Here, take it."

I put on the round-collared biker jacket and zip it up halfway. I immediately feel much warmer.

"Huh. Perfect fit. Looks better on you than it does on me, too," he says, crossing his arms.

"Everything looks better on me."

"I'll pretend I didn't hear that. And this is for you to occupy your time while you're here." He hands me a worn book and a pencil.

"Sudoku. Really?"

"I'm Chinese. What did you expect? I've done all the hard ones, so I don't think I'll need to mop your brain off the floor when I return. I gotta get back to work. Have fun."

The sleeve squeaks when I wave him away. I study the jacket closer. It feels heavier than my leather jackets, and stiffer, too. Parts of the worn surface near the seams have flaked off. I shake my head, amused. It's not even genuine leather. I lean back, pull the collar up, and inhale deeply. The lemon body wash scent is there, mixed with coffee and road dust. And something else. Deeper, baser. I steal a glance at Jacen. He's clearing off a table at the other end of the cafe.

My heart slows down a little. I feel calmer, somehow.

I'm cracking my head over my ninth puzzle when Jacen returns, this time empty-handed.

"Azraai, sorry, but we're closing in ten minutes," he says.

I look up at him. "What time is it?"

"11:49."

I let out a heavy sigh. "Just when you guys started operating twenty-four hours, this Covid thing happened."

"At least we don't have to close at eight anymore," he says.

"Hey. Is it okay if I stay here for a bit while you guys clean up? I don't want to go home just yet."

Jacen taps his mask. "Shouldn't be a problem. I'll tell the assistant manager. But you have to do something in return."

"Like what?"

Jacen leaves with my question unanswered. He goes from table to table to remind other customers that they're closing soon. I'm curious, but I feign nonchalance by tackling the sudoku puzzle. Once the last customer has left, one of the baristas replaces the overhead ambient music with The Weeknd's "Blinding Lights" and cranks up the volume. Most of them dance while they clear off the display counter and tilt the chairs against their respective tables.

When Jacen comes out of the staff room, he carries an old guitar. "Here. Play a song while we clean up."

"But The Weeknd's playing."

Jacen signals for one of the female baristas to kill the music.

Everyone pauses to look at us.

"Where did you even get this?" I ask. I turn the guitar over to study it. The fretboard is littered with pale nail indentations, and overlapping stickers fill the front and back surfaces of the body. A capo is clamped at the edge of the headstock. The pegs squeal when I turn them to tune the guitar. Not that I need to adjust much. I can immediately tell how well-loved it is.

"Some senior left it in the changing room when he quit years ago. So the guys who can play have been maintaining it, changing the strings and all."

"Why don't you play it?" I ask.

Jacen holds up both hands. "I don't even know how to hold it right."

I pluck the strings absently, not knowing what to play. Taking off the jacket, I pull the capo from the headstock and then clamp it over the second fret. I pluck the cords, softly at first, and then with more conviction.

I launch into the song.

I finish the outro as softly as I started the intro. When I look up, I discover that everyone has stopped working to give me their full attention. Even Jacen, who's leaning against the cashier counter with his mask off, stares at me with slack jaws.

Someone claps. The rest follow.

"It was like watching an MV," says one girl. "Some people just have it all. It's so unfair."

Her fellow baristas laugh and resume cleaning. The Weeknd picks up where he left off. I fiddle with the guitar while they work.

After a while, Jacen comes to my table bearing two paper cups filled with hot drinks. Steam wafts off the open cups. He sits opposite me and leans back. He blows on his drink before taking a sip. "Hot chocolate with a bit of cinnamon powder. Low-fat milk, no cream. Maybe it's a bit sweet for your liking, but I don't care," he says.

I take my cup and hold it with both hands, appreciating its warmth. "Thanks. You still owe me a meal, by the way. This doesn't count."

"I thought you weren't serious about it. We forgot to exchange numbers, so I followed your Instagram and DMed you my number, but you never replied. I figured you were not interested."

"I never open my DMs. And I get new followers almost every day. I've stopped checking the notifications and comments."

"So famous."

"What to do? What's your handle, anyway? I'll check when I get home."

"Zhenxinquan2001."

I raise both eyebrows.

Jacen guffaws. "Don't judge. I was in Form Three in Chinese school when I created the account. Jacen didn't exist yet."

Seeing that most of the baristas have left, I get up and return Jacen's jacket. "Thanks for lending me this and for the drink. I'll WhatsApp you my number."

"Sure thing. Hey, what was the song just now? I've never heard it before."

"'Always'. Francois Klark."

"It's a beautiful song."

"I know."

"You sang it beautifully."

"I know."

Jacen chuckles and shakes his head. "Good night, Azraai. Drive safe."

I raise my cup at him. "Thanks again for this."

When I reach home, all the lights have been switched off except for the ones in the hallway and staircase. I latch the front door as quietly as possible. Mak Su's room is downstairs, and she's a light sleeper. Knowing her, she'll wake up to reheat dinner for me even though it's almost two. And she'd stay up until I finished eating.

My phone is on the bed. The home screen shows incoming messages from Vidya, a few other friends, and Mak Su. She rarely WhatsApps me. I ignore the messages and open my I-G instead.

Scrolling through my list of followers will be a futile effort, so I type in @zhenxinquan2001 in the search bar. Jacen's account has been set to private. He has 56 followers, and he follows 327 accounts, including mine. I tap on the blue 'Follow' bar and then toss the phone back on the bed.

It dings right after it lands.

I pick the phone up. On the home screen, Instagram's push notification states, "JACEN QUAN (zhenxinquan2001) accepted your follow request. Now you can see their photos and videos."

There goes my sleep.

6

It's funny how social media is their digital footprint with some people, while with others, it only adds to their mystery. Vidya chronicles almost everything, including that one time she had a yeast infection. But what she shares is what she wants the world to see: a wealthy socialite and model who travels to all the exotic parts of the world and eats amazing foods. What she doesn't share is so much more. She doesn't post intimate pictures of the girls she dates, and she seldom finishes the meals she shares under the foodporn hashtag. Her I-G is as carefully curated as she is, which says a lot, but only if you get to know her in person.

At least those who follow Vidya's account get a taste of her life. Jacen said he created his account when he was in Form Three, but he has only posted 214 photos in the past four years. Other than a few shots of him and his friends in school uniform, his face barely appears in his feed. Most of the posts are in black and white and show random things like grilled shop fronts, random people eating at stalls or walking in the street, plant life, and stray animals. Not that the photos are in any way terrible; in fact, he has a keen eye for lighting and composition. But there's nothing about his family, hobbies, or hints of him as a person. The posts have minimal or no captions, and not a single hashtag.

"There's nothing, Vid. No posts that show he has or had a girlfriend," I say, showing Vidya Jacen's I-G profile on my phone.

She looks at the screen with obvious disinterest before returning her attention to her I-G feed. "Boyfriend?"

"Nope. Besides, he has this straight vibe you can spot from any distance."

Vidya nods without looking up. "That he does. Babe, you've been obsessing over his Insta feed for the past three days. You'll end up deep-liking one of his posts by accident."

Vidya drops her phone on the table and sits straighter when I keep quiet. She locks me up with her hazel eyes. No matter how much I squirm, I can't seem to escape.

"You poor, poor boy. You did, didn't you? How far back was it?"

"I don't know. From two years ago, I think," I mumble. Then, I blurt out, "But I canceled the like."

"Babe, that's irrelevant. He'd still get a notification."

I groan and cover my face with both hands. "Damn it, I'm an idiot. I should just unfollow him. I don't think I can face him after this. What if he thinks I'm a stalker?"

Vidya rolls her eyes. She's the only one who can pull it off looking classy.

My phone dings. It's a WhatsApp message from Jacen. I show the notification to Vidya without reading it first. "What should I do?"

"Read it? Why are you getting all worked up? I thought you don't go for straight boys?"

She's right. I should squash all hope before it takes root. I open the app and read his message.

[Jacen]: Want to grab something to eat that's under RM200? I'm free today from 3 to 7 pm.

I smile when I read the message aloud, but one look from Vidya breaks the spell. For a few seconds, anyway, because another message comes in, and I'm smiling again.

[Jacen]: This is Jacen.

"You're setting yourself up for disappointment," Vidya says, glancing at me from the corner of her eyes.

"It's just a meal, Vid. Any recommendations?"

"Do you want to impress him or scare him away?"

"I don't follow," I say.

"If it's just a meal, like what you said, any mamak joint will do. Besides, it's not like you're planning to go on a second date."

"It's not a date."

Vidya dismisses my comment with a wave. "If you want to impress him, go someplace within your element where you can show him who you are."

I can think of a few places that fit her description. "And what will scare him away?"

"Bring him to places *I* would go. Don't look, but a girl is coming this way. If she asks for a selfie with you, don't be a drama queen and just do it. She's not interested in you, anyway."

I lean closer, intrigued. "How can you tell?"

"She's been making eye contact with me since her group walked in. Now be cool."

Before I can think of a comeback, the girl in question approaches our table and asks for a selfie with me. She's pretty and petite, and she wears her black blouse and cream flared pants well. Her dyed hair is set in a loose bun. She looks Chinese, but I'm not surprised if she has a fancy English name.

When Vidya instructs the girl to stand closer, she scoots behind me, but unlike most of my 'fans', she doesn't come so close that I'm forced to breathe the air she exhales. Vidya's right. She doesn't seem to be genuinely interested in me.

After a couple of shots, Vidya returns the girl's phone. "I accidentally took a photo using the front-facing camera. I like that shot, actually. Can you WhatsApp me the photo if I give you my number?"

Once the girl is beyond hearing range, I snicker at Vidya. "Smooth, Vid. Real smooth. Now stay here and watch over my things. Bio break."

Vidya's phone dings. She waves me away without looking up. I can't believe her tactic works. I'm still chuckling when I enter the male toilet. A guy is washing his hands, but otherwise, the place is empty. I pee at one of the urinals. I notice the guy's reflection glaring right at me when I'm done. Unlike Vidya's situation, I don't think he intends to exchange numbers or bodily fluids with me.

Ignoring him, I wash my hands two sinks away. He doesn't quite reach my nose, and he doesn't look like a gym rat. I can easily take him on if I have to.

"You're disgusting," says his reflection. If not for his threatening sneer, I'd find him attractive, in an asshole-bigoted-Malay kind of way.

Who am I kidding? An asshole, literal or figurative, is *never* attractive.

"You'll burn in hell for the things you do. For what you are."

I pretend really hard to ignore him while I study his face. He looks familiar. I think he's the same guy who saw me in the basement toilet and then catcalled me in front of Jacen. I walk up to him and use my height to my full advantage. He backs away half a step, but I've forced him to look at me directly.

"Either hit me or hit on me. I don't have the time to entertain both," I say. I lean closer, turn off his tap, and walk away without looking back.

I only realize I've been holding my breath and my hands in tight knuckles when I return to my seat. Vidya immediately sits straighter, her full attention on me.

"Babe, what's wrong?"

Vidya's perceptive, but so am I. I know she was smiling to herself before I returned to our table, likely flirting with the girl from just now. "Nothing. So give me some ideas about where to meet Jacen already. Someplace impressive that won't scare him away."

I sent Jacen the location of a local coffee shop at Jalan Tun H.S. Lee. It's more of a hipster bistro with Instragrammable food that's under thirty ringgits. I've hung out here a few times with my school friends around the time we took our SPM, but this is my first time since before the pandemic.

I scan the bistro's QR code to check-in and then get my temperature taken at the entrance. Once inside, I look around to see if Jacen has arrived ahead of me. He's sitting at a small table for two next to the wall in front of the counter. Framed artworks from local artists fill the wall. The illuminated name of the bistro on the granite wall above the counter and the hanging ceiling lamp cast an orange glow, which is made more prominent by the late afternoon sunlight filtered through the tinted floor-to-ceiling glass wall opposite the framed artworks. In a loose white T-shirt and black jeans, Jacen completes the aesthetics. I fight the urge to capture this moment using my phone.

Jacen sees me and raises his hand. I wave back.

"Did you wait long? Sorry, it's near impossible to get a parking spot here," I say. I take the seat across from Jacen.

He smiles and attempts to lean back, but the cramped space restricts his movement. He positions his chair obliquely so that he can freely stretch his legs a little. "Five, ten minutes ago. This is why I prefer riding a motorbike to move around KL. Do you come here often? I've heard about this place, but this is my first time here."

I signal for the waiter to bring us the menu. "I like the vibe. Fewer people compared to Starbucks, and the food is good," I say.

"Not as noisy, too."

"There's that. Are you sure you're paying for this? I'm hungry. I intend to eat a lot."

Jacen pats his seasoned leather wallet on the table. "You saved my skin during the photoshoot. This is the least I can do," he says.

I order the spicy prawn Aglio olio, while Jacen chooses the smashed burger. When I order an iced Americano, he raises an eyebrow at me.

"You love your coffee, huh?" he asks.

"Don't you?"

"Only in the mornings. I prefer chocolate drinks." Then, looking at the waiter, he says, "A glass of warm water for me, please."

I came here prepared to spend extended periods of awkward silence, but Jacen has a different idea, apparently. As soon as the waiter walks away, he leans back again and crosses his arms. He's not at all shy at maintaining eye contact.

"So what's your deal? How come you look like you?" he asks. Straight to the point.

I fold my sleeves to just below my elbows. "My dad's Malay, but with Chinese-Thai blood. My mom was half Dutch."

"I'm sorry."

"She passed away a long time ago," I say in a dismissive tone.

"You got your eyes from your mom, then?"

My eyes are light brown with green flecks, almost unheard of among the Malay community. They set me apart, along with my natural chestnut wavy curls. "That's what I'm told," I mumble. A blank face obscured by bright light appears whenever I think about her. To shake the unsettling image off, I steer the conversation toward Jacen. "What about you? What's your deal? I don't hear the surname Quan often."

"My ancestors were generals and warriors during one of the Chinese dynasties."

"Really?" I ask, impressed.

Jacen guffaws, not seeming to care about the looks he gained. "No. I came from a long line of farmers as far as I know. My great-grandparents migrated here, hoping for a better life."

"They should have gone to the US instead," I say.

"It's not so bad here. Good food, good company. Next question: how big is your family?"

I give him a half-smile. "Is this an interview? It's gonna cost you more than a meal."

Jacen matches my smile. I honestly don't know who wears it better. "Come on, indulge me. I want to be a journalist, so this is good practice."

"Only if it's off-record."

Jacen raises his right hand. His face is serious, but his eyes are smiling. "Promise," he says.

"Only child. You?"

"I have four younger siblings."

"Isn't that…" I say, trailing off.

"Big for a Chinese family? I know. But I like it. I want to have a big family too, one day."

His words are not lost on me, but the more we talk, the more I want to get to know him. I sit back and stretch my legs. We accidentally touch, but Jacen doesn't seem to notice. He asks me one question after another: how long have I been modeling, and do I like it? Why did I choose business studies? How often do I hang out at Starbucks, and do I have other spots? Who's the girl I always hang out with? Is she my girlfriend?

"Vidya? You can call her that. She keeps things interesting," I say.

Vidya and I have an understanding. If people ask us whether we're a couple, the answer is yes. It makes for a great alibi to cover our separate extracurricular activities.

Our food arrives before Jacen can ask any follow-up questions. The presentation is commendable, especially Jacen's burger, which is placed on a rectangular wooden slab. I immediately spear my spaghetti with a fork, but he stops me with a question.

"You're not going to take a picture and post it on social media first?"

I can't tell if Jacen's being sarcastic or genuinely curious. "My posts are an endorsement," I say. When Jacen's face reflects incomprehension, I add, "I have over 300,000 followers. Any place or product I post on my I-G promotes it. People usually offer to pay me to advertise their brand."

"You're an influencer. Got it," he says.

"I wouldn't call myself that. And I don't do sponsored ads. Vidya does, though."

"But it's good money."

I shrug at this. "I guess. But I usually post things I like."

"Your posts are mostly just you, though," he says.

So Jacen has browsed through my feed. Interesting. I lean forward and give him my most disarming smile. "What can I do? I love myself the most. But it's also what people want to see."

Business is all about opportunity, and this is mine. I take out my phone and compose my shot, with Jacen as the centerpiece. He raises his eyebrows but says nothing. I snap a photo and then show it to him.

"Here. Switch places for a bit. Can you take a shot of me like this? Include the bistro's name on that wall."

Jacen does as he's told. Sitting on his chair, I unbutton my shirt halfway down, lean back, stretch my left leg, place my right hand beside the burger, rest my left elbow on the armrest, and then bite the tip of my thumbnail. I part my lips a little and look out at the glass wall. Jacen moves the other chair aside and kneels on one leg to compose his shot. After a few snaps, he returns my phone, and we switch back to our original seats.

I look at the photos and give a low whistle. The composition is brilliant, almost like a magazine spread. He's even got the lighting to perfection. I use an app to convert the best shot into black and white, and tweak the contrast a little before posting it on I-G with the caption "good food, good company." I also tag the bistro. Within seconds, the likes come flooding in.

Jacen checks his phone. "You've gotta be kidding. Over a thousand likes already? And look at the comments. Hey, wait. Isn't this what I said just now?"

"Thanks for the photo and the caption. I'd tag you, but that'll mean I'm endorsing you, too," I say.

"Never mind me. I still don't see how you're endorsing the burger."

"*I'm* the product. I'm the feature in the photo. But since I included the bistro and the food, they get free promotion. It's good for their business. You'll understand soon. Now eat," I say, twirling my spaghetti.

Jacen looks skeptical, but he grabs his burger with both hands and takes a large bite. The fork and knife lie untouched. I smother a smile. I thought I was the only one who ate burgers like this, even at posh restaurants.

While we eat, the phone beside the cash register rings repeatedly, and more customers trickle in. Soon enough, the bistro becomes almost as noisy as a Starbucks outlet, but Jacen doesn't seem to care. He continues to ask me random questions between mouthfuls of the burger. Once we finish our food, the waiter replaces our empty plates with a slice of brownie topped with vanilla ice cream.

"We didn't order any dessert," says Jacen.

I sit back to enjoy this better.

"Compliments of the house," says the waiter.

"We're not celebrating anyone's birthday."

The waiter's eyes dart between Jacen and me. Even though his face is partially hidden behind a surgical mask, it's evident that Jacen has put him in an awkward position. He excuses himself and comes back with a middle-aged man who carries himself far more confidently than the waiter.

"I hope you enjoyed your meal. Please accept this dessert. I insist," he says.

"Why?" Jacen asks.

"We wondered why we suddenly received a lot of phone inquiries and online orders. And as you can see, we're almost at full capacity. Then we saw your Instagram post tagging us. I hope you don't mind if we repost it."

Smiling behind curled fingers, I give the manager a nod of consent.

"Thanks. And please, enjoy the brownie," he says before backing away.

Looking at Jacen's dumbfounded expression, I smile wider. "Now, do you understand why I don't post just anything?"

"You're an influencer," he says, his tone almost accusatory.

"I still won't call myself that. People say I'm a bad influence."

Jacen's laugh fills the bistro. "I've never met a celebrity before. I think you're my first. So, are we sharing this?"

"You go ahead. I don't like sweet things."

Speaking of celebrities, a group of girls approaches our table just as Jacen is about to finish the brownie. All of them look our age, maybe younger. They've been looking our way and nudging one another at the table just outside the glass wall since they came here. I was wondering if they'd do it.

"Hi, Azraai. Do you mind if we take a picture with you?" says the leader of the group.

"Just me or with my friend over here, too?" I ask, more amused by Jacen's reaction than by the request.

"Just you," she says, but someone else chimes in, "But my friend wants to take a picture with him."

I quickly scan the group, and sure enough, one of the girls looks down, her cheeks and ears a bright shade of red. She's a pretty Chinese girl, almost as fair as Jacen, and her long coppery hair is tied in a neat ponytail. Her outfit is simple: a white printed T-shirt and a pair of distressed jeans. Vidya would definitely be interested. I glance at Jacen, and he looks at me, wide-eyed.

One of the taller girls whips out a selfie stick and positions her phone to include all of us in the frame. Jacen shuffles his chair back to give us space, but I catch him stealing glances at the girl who's interested in him. After a few poses, the girls thank me and then leave. The still-blushing girl is the first to rush away.

"She wanted a picture with you," I say.

Jacen stares at the exit, where the girls are. He says nothing.

"You don't want to disappoint her, do you? Go. Take a picture with her."

The girls exit the bistro. Jacen surges up, almost toppling his chair, and then chases after the girl.

"Get her number, too," I say, louder than necessary.

Straight boys. They can be so clueless sometimes.

7

These past two weeks have been crazy tight. Not only do I have to cram for an upcoming quiz on top of a group presentation, the boutique that booked me a few times last year called my agent three days ago for a photoshoot to promote their latest collection of wedding lines. The idiot agent said yes without consulting me first, as usual. I could have said no when he sprang this on me, but I needed the distraction. Also, it's been a while since I met up with the other models the boutique likes to book.

They've rented some rich guy's mansion for the photoshoot. It has the requisite white walls and high ceiling, a curved staircase with a broad base, roman pillars, Victorian furniture, and lush greeneries that likely require a gardener just to manage the indoor plants. After coming home from Turkey or something, the owner and his family are quarantined at some five-star hotel, so only the housekeepers are around to greet us and make sure we don't steal or break anything.

The boutique has booked ten talents, five girls, and five guys. The bride, her groom, and the rest will be bridesmaids and dulang boys entourage. Like previous sessions, we were not informed beforehand who would be chosen as the principal models. Still, in my experience, they always chose Zakry, a model five years my senior who's a perfect blend of Malay and Caucasian.

Also, in my experience, he's good with his perfect mouth and hands, and he looks way better without clothes.

When all the talents have arrived and Zakry is not among them, I ask around, but none of the models have an answer. Our general assumption is that he's either contracted the coronavirus or he's under quarantine. Or he's so paranoid about getting the virus that he's given this job a pass.

The boutique staff, makeup artists, and camera crew arrived ahead of us, but everyone has to wait for Dato' Hanis, the boutique owner, to arrive before we can start. And that woman loves to make an entrance. When the housekeeper opens the gigantic double doors, she sashays in and greets us with a forced American accent. She wears a form-fitting kebaya top and a pair of white jeans, and her square sunglasses cover half her face. Her lips definitely look much plumper than what I remember.

"Look at you beautiful children. I am inspired, truly," she says. At least she never pretends to be someone half her age.

Dato' Hanis stops in the middle of the hall, looks around, and lowers her sunglasses to undress us one by one with her eyes. She walks up to me, grabs my arms to turn me around twice, and then steps back to study me as if I were a painting on a wall.

"Azraai. It's a shame what happened, but you'll be my new Zakry. I must say, you're glowing up nicely. Even if Zakry were here, I would have still chosen you to be the groom. Maybe. Especially if you buff up a bit more, you know. Now get ready, all of you," she says, clapping her manicured hands.

That's the fashion industry for you. There will always be someone younger and better, ready to take your place at any given time.

While the chief photographer consults Dato' Hanis, the boutique staff ushers us upstairs for costume fitting and makeup. They lead the girls to a room at the end of the hall, and the boys are in the opposite one. From the looks of the ostentatious furnishing, I'm guessing this is a guest room.

We strip to our underwear while the staff picks the right clothes for us to don. The other four models are much more buffer than I am, but none of them have my height or skin tone. The staff hands me a white double-faced satin baju Melayu after taking out the shoulder pads. The cool fabric glides on my skin as I put it on. The top accents my deltoids and pecs, but the staff applies pins at the sides to make them hug my waist even more snugly. It's funny how baju kurung is getting more elaborate and hides the female figure, but baju Melayu designs are getting tighter to reveal the muscular form.

I sit at the edge of the king-sized bed as a makeup artist attends to my face. I don't usually pay attention to whoever's doing my makeup, but this particular artist is a fascinating juxtaposition. He wears thick makeup complete with lash extensions, smoky eyeshadows, and face contouring, but he also sports decent facial hair. His hair is in a topknot. He has a rugby player's shoulders, but his low-cut V neck boasts some cleavage. He also insists that I call him 'Sis' in that deep voice of his.

Since he's also chatty, I decide to try my luck by asking about Zakry. A subtle shift in the room's atmosphere tells me that everyone else is also listening in.

The makeup artist clicks his tongue. "You don't know about the video?"

"What video?"

"Look up. Anyone ever told you that you have cute freckles? So you didn't hear this from me, but someone leaked his sex video on Pornhub."

"So?" I ask. Once in a while, news about local celebrities' leaked sex or jerk-off videos will surface. While they can end a female artist's career, a male celebrity usually brushes off these reports and will claim that the photos or videos are deepfake even when it's blatantly him, and life goes on.

The makeup artist clicks his tongue again. "Dik, the video's in the gay category. Zakry was having sex with some unknown twink."

"Was he top or bottom? You have the video, don't you, Sis?" one model asks.

"A guy like him? A top, of course. I'm not telling or sharing anything with you perverts, but I can tell you it's hot," says the makeup artist. He laughs and pats my thigh, a little too close to my groin.

He's wrong, by the way. Zakry is versatile. But this news hits me hard. I can safely bet that half this room are gays, bis, or at least curious, but in this country, it's something you can never advertise. Nothing kills a promising career faster than hard proof of gay sexual encounters. I fight the urge to text Zakry to check up on him. We're not friends, and he was stupid to record himself having sex, but he doesn't deserve this.

"What happens now?" I ask, more to myself.

The makeup artist dabs highlight from the bridge to the tip of my nose. "Well, from what I heard, his agency dropped him, his fans turned on him, and no one will book him for the next few years at least. He might as well say goodbye to his modeling days," he says.

That sucks big time. Zakry doesn't have wealthy parents to be his safety net. Maybe I will check up on him later. For now, I need to concentrate on doing well, or this will be my only time as the principal model for this boutique.

Once the makeup is done, the boutique staff takes over to accessorize me. He pins one end of a silver link chain on my right shoulder, and the other at the top edge of my left chest pocket. He then slots in pearl-studded silver buttons right up to my collar before putting on a stiff white songket sampin with finely woven silver threads around my waist. I run my fingers over the silver bamboo shoots and pastel pink and blue flowers motifs, admiring the masterful craftsmanship.

"This is beautiful. How much is it?" I ask.

"It's an original Terengganu handwoven songket. The selling price is eight thousand ringgit, so be careful not to snag or stain it."

I immediately lift my hands and let the staff fold and fasten the sampin. Once he's satisfied, the staff chooses a plain black songkok and fits it on my head. I then put on black leather shoes before the makeup artist adds the finishing touches. After everyone's done, the staff members managing us usher us back downstairs.

As expected, the girls are nowhere near ready. The photographer takes shots of the guys first. He instructs me to stand at the base of the staircase, and the other guys, all in uniform baju Melayu with gray songket sampin, to flank me from behind in a pyramid formation. While he does test shots, Dato' Hanis enters the hall and saunters up to me. She straightens the creases on my shoulders and adjusts my songkok.

"Your baju Melayu design and sampin are magnificent," I say, more to calm my nerves.

"Darling, *you* make the ensemble magnificent. I can't wait to see you and the bride together. I know you were special from the first time I booked you, you know." she says.

"Thanks."

Dato' Hanis leans closer and whispers for my ears alone. "I know you don't do girls. I don't care. As long as you don't pull a Zakry, I'll care for you. Understood?"

She could have shouted those words, and it wouldn't have made a difference. Her warning comes across chillingly loud.

One of the male models texts me to hook up after the shoot. We did it once before. The bride and her friend want to hang out. After learning about Zakry and hearing Dato' Hanis's thinly veiled threat, I don't feel horny or sociable. And since the old man is not working today, I don't intend to go home until well after his bedtime. Which is why I'm waiting in line to place my order at my favorite joint. The crowd is not too bad since it's almost dinnertime, but the traffic outside is a nightmare.

Jacen greets me at the counter. "Hi, welcome to Starbucks. What can I get for you today?"

I look up from my phone and raise both eyebrows. I'm not even wearing a mask today. "It's me. Azraai."

His mask moves up as he smiles. He makes a circular gesture around his face. "I know. But you look different."

I blink a few times before realizing what he meant. "Oh. I had a photoshoot just now, and the makeup artist did a superb job. It's a shame to wash it off there and then. Too much?"

"I don't think any of the girls here will be able to sleep tonight. Don't be surprised if the baristas ask for a picture with you as the girls did at the bistro. Can you do me a favor and not tag this place with you looking like this? I'm looking forward to a chill evening."

I scoff at Jacen. "No promises."

"So what will it be? The usual?"

"Yeah. Wait. No. Do you remember that drink I ordered before?"

Jacen doesn't even attempt to give it a thought. "Vanilla latte, extra shot. Less ice, no sugar, and low-fat milk. Got it. Lasagna or mushroom soup? Or something else?"

I must have been gaping like an idiot because he has to clear his throat. I clamp my mouth and give him a nod. "Yeah, that one. And lasagna, please."

He writes my order on the transparent venti cup. We look at each other for a few seconds before he lowers his mask to grin at me directly. "Azraai, it's 31.90. Cash or card?"

"Oh. Sorry." I fumble to retrieve my wallet from my back pocket and almost drop it. The packet of condoms I keep in my wallet slips out. Hoping that no one sees it, I immediately push the foil packet back.

Once the payment is complete, Jacen hands me the receipt. "Thank you. I'll send your food shortly. Stay safe." He adds the last one with a smirk.

If I wasn't blushing before, I'm doing it now. I retreat to a quiet corner before I embarrass myself further. Once I've settled down, I check out the pictures the assistant photographer helped take using my phone. Most of them are pretty good. I can't use the official photos on my I-G, and the unofficial ones in costume are also out of bounds until the boutique has released its promotional blasts and gives us the green light. Still, Dato' Hanis has given me her blessing to post one particular photo, with the condition that I tag her boutique. Quid pro quo. She told me that it'd be good for her and me, but I'm sure she's getting the better end of the deal with the number of followers I have.

I post the photo of the closeup of the bride leaning on my chest, and we're looking at each other. It has that intimate newlywed vibe, and likes and comments come flooding in as soon as the picture is up. Most of them are heart emojis. Some even give heartbreak and cry emojis. I guess this is one way Dato' Hanis is taking care of me.

A sudden screech followed by a crash shatters the din of the cafe. People surge from their chairs to rush outside to where the noise source is. Even the baristas join in. But I don't need to leave my seat to know what that noise implies.

I've lived through it.

The sky is a brilliant shade of blue. I remembered seeing something similar on cold autumn mornings in Paris where my parents took me the previous year, but never here in KL. My mom was crying as she drove, so I made as little noise as possible in the passenger seat. I didn't know what was making her sad. I held my toy space shuttle up and pretended it was flying across the cloudless sky, over treetops, and between tall buildings. My eyes darted everywhere but at my mom. I hated seeing her cry.

It was my fault my mom cried so much. It was my fault my dad was angry with me all the time. I just couldn't understand why.

"He's wrong. He's wrong. You're my perfect boy. He's wrong," she mumbled between sobs.

There were things an eight-year-old's mind couldn't comprehend, and this was one of them. One thing I understood was the fear. I gripped the shuttle tighter, wishing I was inside it, flying far away from here.

Buildings zoomed past us — or was it the other way around? I couldn't remember the details; they seemed unimportant. The sky was so big and blue; I searched frantically for a familiar cloud.

I saw it first. I pointed at the oncoming gray SUV as if I had the power to stop time. It rammed into my mom's side like an angry elephant. Maybe this was why I would later become uneasy around these gigantic beasts. Our car flew as it flipped and rolled sideways. The shrill squeaks of the frame bending and the shriek of metal against asphalt exploded in my ears. Within the bubble of the deafening noise, a sudden stillness took over when the engine died and heat expanded from the dashboard. The windscreen cracked in a million places all at once, and as the ground became the sky and the sky gave way to the ground, my space shuttle hung suspended in front of me for a second that lasted forever, as if it were truly flying in zero gravity.

When our car finally stopped rolling, we hung upside down. It was then that I realized my mom's hand had pressed against my chest all that time because when it dropped, slack, I slid from under the seatbelt and thudded against the dented and torn ceiling.

I looked up at her. Her chestnut curls swayed like an old tree's hanging roots, and blood dripped everywhere. Her skirt draped down like a curtain, but red stains quickly spread to cover the white. I only smelled the sharp iron when I saw the blood. The sun's reflection obscured her face in the side mirror.

I called out to her. I croaked her name. I shouted.

Someone reached in and pulled me away. I grabbed the hand that had saved my life, but it would not hold me back. My mom did not hold me back.

I'm on the floor calling out for my mom. I reach out and grab at the air, at nothing. I'm back in the car, hanging upside down, the weight of her phantom hand heavy on my chest. I claw at my shirt, desperate to tear it open, to breathe. The hot dead air expands and pushes against me as if it were a physical force. I kick the floor and push myself back, but something solid stops me. A chair? A pillar?

But I'm still in the car. I pull at the constricting seatbelt, but I can't find it.

I scream for my mom. Why doesn't she answer?

I can't breathe. I can't breathe. Ican'tbreathe. Ican't —

Warm and heavy darkness blankets me. Even breathing through my mouth, I can smell the mixture of lemon, coffee, and road dust. The scent settles in and pushes back the dead heat. It's dark. I can't see anything. I still can't breathe.

And then strong arms wrap around me in a tight embrace. I squirm to get away, but the dark blanket and the bear hug restrict my movements. I kick blindly to set myself free, but the arms loosen their hold just enough to fold my legs and include them in the embrace, too.

A weight presses against my head, and a whispered voice repeats, "It's okay, you're safe," like a mantra.

My body eventually stills. I didn't even realize I was shivering. My breaths come in ragged hiccups, and my face is wet. Was I crying?

Once my body relaxes, so do the arms that hold me.

The blanket finally lifts — only, it's not a blanket, but a leather jacket peeling at the seams. I know the jacket. I know the scent. Waves of comforting heat come from my left. Jacen is on the floor beside me, his long legs encircling me and his lean but muscular arms still holding me in a tight embrace. I blink at him, disoriented and confused. I look around. People are staring at us. Some of them have their phones out and pointed at me.

"There's nothing to see. Please, stop recording," Jacen begs loudly for the entire cafe to hear. Then, pressing his head against mine, he whispers, "It's okay. You're safe."

I breathe slower, deeper. My entire body slackens, and I collapse against him. He catches me and continues his soothing mantra. His chest rumbles with each syllable, and I can feel his strong heartbeat against the side of my head.

"I'm all right," I whisper after what feels like an eternity.

"No, you're not. Can you walk?"

I nod and hoist myself up, using his body as a crutch. My knees buckle, but Jacen jumps up to support me. Before I can say anything, he throws the jacket over my head.

"Wha—"

"You're gonna thank me later," he says as he drags me with such force that my feet automatically follow.

I can tell that we walk past a swinging door and that Jacen stops to lock it before lifting the jacket. I only register where we are after a few fluttered blinks. We're in the toilet. Under a different circumstance, I'd find this arousing, but right now I'm just confused. My face must have conveyed my state of mind because Jacen laughs and points at the mirror. My reflection quickly displays mortification.

"Guess your makeup's not waterproof," he says, still smiling.

I gave a full theatrical production of a full-blown panic attack out there, and he's still concerned about *my face*?

I don't understand Jacen. I really don't.

He pulls out a generous amount of tissue paper from the dispenser beside the mirror and turns on the tap. He holds a piece under running water and then folds it before dabbing my face, starting from my forehead. Using his other hand, he pushes back my hair. The gentle gesture is the exact opposite of when he restrained me, but I'm just as paralyzed now.

If I kiss him, will he push me away? Will he hate me?

"You're not going to ask what happened back there?" I ask softly as he wipes my closed eyelids.

"You'll tell me about it when you're ready. Even if you never tell me, it's all right."

"How did you know what to do, the thing you did back there?"

Jacen applies pressure when he wipes my cheeks, probably because of the smeared mascara rivers. "My brother is autistic. Sometimes he gets this sensory overload when he's in a crowded place he's not familiar with. So I cut him off from the world and let him concentrate on just me."

"Sensory deprivation," I say.

"Something like that. Or focus. I can't remember the name. The therapist taught me what to do whenever my brother gets an anxiety attack. Weird thing is, only this jacket does the trick. Nothing else works on him. That's why I always have it around even when it's a hundred degrees outside."

"Worked on me, too," I say.

"I guess it did."

I wash my face to remove the last remnants of makeup. When I look up, I catch Jacen's reflection looking at me. He meets my eyes and doesn't shy away.

"You gonna be all right?" he asks.

I nod and then wipe my face dry with fresh tissue paper.

"Stay here for as long as you need. I'm going to do some damage control."

"That concerned about my image?"

Giving me a half-smile, Jacen shakes his head. "I told you, I want a relatively quiet shift."

My reflection looks at him as he opens the door. "Hey, Jacen?"

"Yeah?"

"Thank you."

8

Sundays are the worst. The old man doesn't work on Sundays, and while he usually stays in the study, there's always that risk of bumping into him. We've somehow developed an unspoken schedule. He goes to the mosque at 5:30 am for Subuh prayer and stays there until 10 for some weekend religious class or something. I go out for a run at 7, have breakfast at 9 after a shower (8:30 if I feel like chatting with Mak Su over the meal), and by the time the old man returns, I'm already safe in my room. My friends sleep in during the weekend, so making plans with them before 2 pm is no use. I usually immerse myself in games, either on my laptop or console. Lunchtime can be tricky, but I often use the game as an excuse to eat after the old man. Mak Su likes to wait for me, but I suspect she does it to guilt me into eating earlier because she sometimes complains about gastric pain. Evenings are not so bad, because the old man goes to the mosque at 7 pm for Maghrib prayer and stays until after Isya', so I have free rein of the house.

But the pandemic has thrown that delicately balanced schedule out the window. The two months during lockdown were a total hell of awkward encounters and near-confrontations. Not to mention all the meals we were forced to eat together in heavy silence. We saw each other more in those two months than in the last five years jumbled together. While he has now gone back to the mosque for Subuh, the morning classes are still a no-go, so he's usually back by 7 am, which sends my breakfast schedule out of whack. I've had the misfortune of bumping into him reading a newspaper in the living room when I got back from my run, and Mak Su forced us to have breakfast together.

I still hate Sundays, but I miss the old norm. This new norm sucks big time.

Vidya finally returns my text as I'm about to leave my teammate to die. He's some random player the game match-made in my team, and he keeps bitching over voice chat, so he's been getting on my nerves. Letting him die is the best I can do, considering you can't kill your teammates in this game.

```
[Vidya] : good morning 2 u 2
[Me] : It's almost 1, Vid.
[Vidya] : u're the only crazy one 2 wake up at ungodly
hours
[Me] : So have you?
[Vidya] : I haven't had my morning coffee. No weird news
about u. Should there be anything?
[Me] : …
[Me] : no

[Jacen] : Azraai, do you have plans today?
[Jacen] : It's me, Jacen.

[Me] : Vid, Jacen just texted me.
[Vidya] : I really need that coffee. Do u need to tell me
every time he texts u?
[Me] : …

[Me] : I saved your number, Jacen. No need to keep
informing me.
[Jacen] : Sorry.
[Me] : Waddup?
[Jacen] : Want to catch a movie?
[Me] : Like on a date?
[Jacen] : …
[Jacen] : Haha. No? I kinda need a wingman.

[Me] : He wants me to be his wingman.
[Vidya] : COFFEE! Don't be an idiot. Say no.

[Me] : Wingman?
[Jacen] : Remember that girl at the bistro? We're going
out but she's bringing a friend.
[Me] : Don't you have friends for that?
[Jacen] : Ouch. I thought we were friends.
[Me] : …

[Me] : Have you had your coffee? I need your advice.
```

```
[Vidya] : no
[Me] : Coffee or advice?
[Vidya] : the answer is no. Don't do it

[Jacen] : Sorry I asked. Just that her friend asked about
you. And I've never done something like this. My friends
will tease me nonstop.
[Me] : jk about that friend thing.
[Jacen] : Got it.
[Me] : …
[Me] : Text me the time and location. You're buying
popcorn.
[Jacen] : I thought models don't eat?
[Me] : This one does.
[Jacen] : Haha. See you there. And thanks!

[Vidya] : u said yes, didn't u
[Vidya] : babe
[Vidya] : AZRAAI
[Me] : ttyl
[Vidya] : u're hopeless
```

And that is how I end up at IOI City Mall some thirty kilometers from home. Not that I mind; I needed an excuse to get out of the house, anyway. The mall is so packed, with actual lines of people waiting to enter food and clothing outlets. It's giving me goosebumps, and not the good kind. I've never given crowded places much thought before, and I always loved being lost among an ocean of people, but these past few months have changed everything so much. Maybe too much.

Navigating the mall is easy when you're much taller than the average Southeast Asia person. It's also easy to spot someone your height. Jacen is leaning against a pillar. He's wearing his faux leather jacket. Maybe he was just flattering me when he said I looked better in it because he looks damn near perfect even with a gray mask on.

Jacen doesn't seem to notice my presence. I stand close and watch him slay another player in a battle arena game on his phone. He only looks up when the opponent kills him.

"You never stood a chance," I say.

"My teammates suck. They always run away first. I hate random matchmakings during weekends," he says and puts his phone away.

"You're not going to finish the game?"

Jacen shrugs. "We're gonna lose, anyway. Besides, you're already here."

"Is it a ranked match?"

"Yeah."

"Are you crazy? Do you want to get a penalty for leaving halfway? Finish the game."

"You sure?"

I nod and lean against the pillar beside him. He takes his phone out and resumes the match after reconnecting. When the battle escalates into a team fight, I lean close and point out an enemy sneaking up on him. Not that he needs any help. One opponent disconnects, and Jacen's team ends up winning despite having all their defensive turrets destroyed.

Jacen turns to look at me. "That was unexpected."

"Hey, a win's a win. And your healer gets the MVP title. What's there to complain?"

"A healer with the most kill count. The team sucked."

"Big-time," I say.

I look around. Despite the packed mall, the cinema is somehow empty. The ticket counters are unmanned, and only one staff is on standby to assist customers at the self-serve kiosks. Even the line at the concession stand is nowhere near as long as those in front of shoe boutiques.

"The girls are not here yet?" I ask.

Jacen checks his phone and types something. It dings almost immediately. He then shows me the screen, both eyebrows raised. It's a photo of the two of us with our backs on the pillar, with me pointing at his phone. I didn't realize we were standing that close.

Two girls approach us with excitement in their steps. One of them is vaguely familiar. She's wearing a black floral print spaghetti strap sundress with a white T-shirt underneath, and a pair of white tennis shoes. Her coppery brown hair is tied in a ponytail, and her side bangs fall over her white mask. Her friend is in a long-sleeved white shirt, shin-length jeans, and cream loafers. While masks give me a semblance of anonymity, they make it damn near impossible to appreciate another person's face.

The girl in the sundress waves at us. "Hi, Jacen, Azraai. Hope you didn't wait for us long."

"Azraai, this is Elayne Goh, and her friend Kit Wan," Jacen says.

Kit Wan scuttles close and looks up at me. The girls only reach our shoulders. Both her hands are holding her phone close to her chest. Call me paranoid, but I have a strong feeling she's recording this.

"Azraai. I'm a huge fan. I keep all your magazine appearances. That girl in your last Instagram post is gorgeous. Is she your current girlfriend?"

A little too outspoken and upfront. Not creepy at all.

Jacen leans close and whispers, "*Current* girlfriend?"

I shrug and direct my question at Kit Wan. "You're not in that AzraAiNi WhatsApp group, are you?"

She gasps and accidentally slaps her phone over her mask. "It was supposed to be a secret fan club group!"

"Fan club?" Jacen whispers again.

"Whatever you do, don't let me sit next to her," I whisper back with clenched teeth.

Wearing a question on his face, Jacen shows his phone to Elayne.

At least she has the decency to look abashed. "Oh. That. You guys were in the zone. We didn't want to disturb you. What game was it, anyway?"

"Mobile Legends," Jacen says.

"My brother forces me to play it so that he has someone to team up with," she says.

"What's your rank?" I ask.

"Elite 2."

I give a low whistle. "And you said your brother *forced* you to play?"

Elayne blushes and pushes her hair away. "I'm more of a battle royale girl myself."

"Which one?" I ask, genuinely intrigued.

"PUBG."

"Mobile or console?"

"Both."

I nudge Jacen's side with my elbow. "I like her. She's my tribe. Send Jacen your username so he can share it with me. Maybe we'll team up one of these weekends."

"I'm glad you approve," Jacen says. Only, I expected more enthusiasm than this.

The cinema hall seems bigger and colder with mandatory alternate seating. The four of us alone already take up a third of a row. Despite Kit Wan's protests, I politely insist she sit first at one end, followed by Elayne, then Jacen, and I take the last assigned seat. I place my popcorn on the empty chair between Jacen and me, and he puts his popcorn beside mine.

"I'm not sharing mine if you finish yours first," I whisper.

Jacen chuckles. "Got it. Azraai doesn't like sharing."

"Damn right. Especially the things I love."

"Such as?"

I snatch my box and flick a popcorn kernel in my mouth. "I love popcorn."

Jacen chuckles again before giving his full attention to Elayne. They lean toward each other in a whispered conversation. I only catch a little of Jacen's words and muffled laughter, but enough to make me feel like an extra at a photoshoot. I notice Kit Wan trying to get my attention, and I give her a small smile before looking away.

The movie is a Korean romantic comedy flick. While I watch Korean movies and dramas on streaming channels, this is my first cinematic experience. Not that I care; I didn't even bother finding out which show we would watch before agreeing to tag along.

The half of me watching the movie acknowledges that it's a good show, with beautiful cinematography and music. The other half of me, however, is acutely aware of every movement Jacen makes, especially when it is a response to Elayne's body language.

I don't know what I was thinking. Vidya was right, as usual. I shouldn't have done this. Maybe I wanted to hang out with Jacen one more time so that I could catch his flaws to make me like him less. Maybe I wanted to check out the girl he likes to catch her flaws to make me dislike her more. I failed on both accounts.

Halfway through the movie, Jacen shifts in his seat, takes off his jacket, and gives it to Elayne for her to put on. I felt special the two times he rescued me with the jacket, but now that warmth is dissipating fast. I was already shivering for the past half-hour, but now I feel much colder. I take out my phone and send Vidya a text.

[Me] : This was a mistake, Vid.
[Vidya] : share ur location babe. Im coming

The most beautiful thing about Vidya that few get to see is that she never says "I told you so" and never rubs it in your face when she's right. She's always there to be your safety net, no questions asked.

9

"As far as days go, today is actually not too bad. I don't know if you're able to see this, but it hasn't rained for five days now, and the sky is so clear, it's starting to get annoying. You would have liked it. You would've told the old man to take a few days off so that the three of us could go on a holiday to enjoy the weather.

"The old man is fine, in case you're wondering. You know better than to expect me to tell you what he's up to. No, I didn't come here to talk about him, okay? You can ask him yourself when he comes to visit. Does he? Visit you?"

The carpet grass on my mom's grave is yellowed from the heat and the dry spell. I fish out fallen leaves from between the fine blades and crumple them in my hand. Throwing them near another person's plot feels rude. Other than the stray leaves, my mom's grave looks impeccable. Even the black granite layered curb surround has a reflective sheen to it. I don't know if the old man pays the cemetery caretaker to maintain the grave or does it himself.

"I'm here because I miss you, Ma. We haven't talked for a while now. Sorry. It's my fault. Been busy with coursework and all. Oh. Last month, something happened, and I remembered more about the accident than I ever did before. But I still couldn't see your face. It's okay because you were bright like the sun. And I remember now that you saved my life.

"Sometimes, I wish you took me with you because life is hard and you're not here. Mak Su does her best, but there are things I cannot tell her. Things I can only share with you."

55

To be fair, my mom is in no position to talk back or chase me out of the house, but an imagined two-sided conversation with my long-dead mother at her grave is something even my therapist would approve of.

"Remember the guy I told you about? Not that one. He was a total idiot. I'm talking about Jacen from college. Yes, the good-looking guy who's my height. He's gorgeous, actually. You have no idea the dreams I've been having...."

I clear my throat. Describing my wet dreams, even when there's no one within earshot, feels inappropriate here. Besides, no sane child talks this freely with their parents, dead or otherwise.

"Anyway. I told myself I'd never fall for a straight boy ever again, but here I am, telling you about the straight boy I've fallen for. He's kind but totally clueless. The effect he has on me, it's not normal, Ma. I want to kiss him whenever I see him, and you know I don't kiss on the lips. The worst thing is, I sorta introduced him to his girlfriend. No, scrap that. The worst worst thing is I kinda like her, too.

"No, Ma. Not like that. Don't be gross. What I'm saying is she's cool. We played online a few times, and she's fantastic. I think if I go up against her, I'll lose for sure. Jacen asked me to be his wingman two weeks ago. Me, a wingman, can you believe that? Seeing them together was rough. They were holding hands when we left the cinema. The last time anyone held my hand was... you."

An errant tear escapes my eyes, and I quickly wipe it away. I don't like letting my mom see me like this. And I don't like this hollow feeling I've harbored since that day.

"I promised Vidya I'd hang out with her today, so I'm going now, Ma. Watch over me like you always do. But look away when I do... stuff, okay?"

I stand up, shove the crumpled leaves in my pocket, dust my pants, and carefully navigate around the closely arranged grave plots to get to the parking lot. I pass by an old couple standing beside a small old grave. The man stoically holds up an umbrella to shade his wife while they recite from a creased Yaasin booklet. His mouth still moving, he looks at me and offers a small nod. I nod back, not quite meeting his eyes. Grief is not something strangers share.

As I reverse my car, I stop long enough to look beyond the couple, toward my mom's grave, and recite al-Fatihah under my breath.

"Of all the places and outlets, you have to choose this one. Why do you keep doing this to yourself, babe?"

I don't answer Vidya. I trace a squiggly line on my plastic cup to connect the condensation beads. The cafe is nearly empty and unusually peaceful, save for two guys in shirts and ties sitting separately but with identical laptops in front of them. Both of them are talking animatedly on their screens. I don't know what their deal is, and I'm not particularly interested to find out, other than noticing them checking out Vidya every once in a while.

Vidya is meticulously made up as if we were going to a posh Michelin restaurant instead of Starbucks, and her turquoise satin cami top accents her skin to perfection. In my defense, I told her beforehand that we were meeting up here, but Vidya is an unstoppable force. She looks around and then focuses on a tall figure walking toward the kitchen.

"Look at that back. I'd appreciate a little more butt, but those skinny jeans are everything. I don't blame you for swooning over that hunk of fine meat," she says after Jacen disappears behind the swinging door.

"I don't swoon. And his butt looks perfect."

Vidya takes a sip from her cup of iced latte. Her nails have been freshly painted white. "Babe, I'm bored."

I let out a small sigh. "I'm sorry, okay? But this has been my haven long before I met him. We can go somewhere else after we finish our drinks."

"No, not that. I'm like really bored right now. It's Friday. We're supposed to be planning which club we'll grace with our presence instead of Netflix and chill at home or hang out at some lame bar or restaurant, as old people do. We're nineteen, for Christ's sake," she says.

"Speaking of, do you Netflix and chill with that girl? Or are you seeing someone new?"

"That's my point exactly. I'm supposed to be at a club grinding against her and other girls, and you're supposed to find other boys to get your mind off Jacen."

"Bring the club to you, then," I say.

"Say what, now?"

I drink my iced Americano and let the idea simmer for a minute. People have started to trickle in, but not enough to generate noise. I kinda like it this way. Once Vidya gives me her exasperated look, I chuckle and sit back. "Clubs can't open. Doesn't mean you can't have a party at your house," I say.

"You're forgetting this Covid thing."

"Politicians have their gatherings. People have weddings. Why can't you have a party at your place? Just limit the number of people you invite, and follow the SOP or whatever. I'm sure your dad can hire some RELA guards and officers. You'll have your dance party, and you and your bae can do whatever it is that girls do."

"Whatever it is that girls do?" Vidya asks. She gives me a grin that only spells trouble.

I hold my hands up and scrunch my face. "No. Don't tell me. Not interested. Unless you want me to describe what *guys* do."

Vidya leans forward, displaying a generous amount of cleavage. "Do tell. Maybe we can compare notes," she says.

"Gross."

"A party at my place. Has anyone ever told you that you're more than just a pretty face?"

Before I can answer, a newcomer catches my attention. I recognize the jacket before I register the person wearing it. I watch as Elayne approaches the counter, says something to the barista, and waits until Jacen comes out of the kitchen. She stands on her toes to kiss him on the cheek.

They're *kissing* now? A sudden draft floods over me, sending me shivering involuntarily.

Vidya swivels in her seat to follow my gaze. "What's happening? Oh… is that her? What's with the oversized jacket? In this weather? That leather is so fake, by the way."

"It's his," I say under my breath. It's his most important possession. And she has it.

"Oh. Sorry. It still doesn't look good on her, though. She's turning this way. Quick, what's her name? Emilia? Elena?"

"Elayne."

"Elayne! Come here, girl," Vidya hollers, catching the entire cafe's attention.

"Vid, what are you doing?" I ask.

Too late. Elayne has spotted us. She walks over to our spot. Jacen cranes his neck to look at me, and I shrug in return. I have no idea what Vidya is playing at. Elayne greets me with a smile and a wave, and then turns her full attention on Vidya.

"I can't believe it's actually you. Vidya Chastain," Elayne says.

"Shas-tan," Vidya says, correcting the pronunciation offhandedly, as if she's been doing it her entire life. Even I got it wrong the first time I read her full name.

"Sorry. I follow your Instagram and Facebook and Twitter. I hope I don't sound like a creepy stalker. You're just so beautiful and glamorous, but you look so much better in person. Your skin is flawless."

This is swooning. I don't recall ever doing it with Jacen. I'm having a hard time accepting this blabbering fangirl as the same person as the online gamer who talks like one of the guys. I make a supreme effort to suppress a cringe. I wonder if this is how Vidya feels whenever a gaggle of girls swarm to get a selfie with me.

Vidya shows off her perfect teeth with a wide smile. She pats the empty chair beside her. "That's so sweet of you. Join us. Babe, you didn't tell me how pretty she is."

"Thanks," Elayne says, fanning herself. Her cheeks have turned red.

"If you end up with Jacen, you'll make good-looking babies," Vidya says. Sometimes her unfiltered mouth worries me.

Elayne's blush spreads to her ears. They are now almost as bright as her hair. "I'm not sure about that. We're just getting to know each other. He wants to take it slow. But the both of you will definitely have beautiful children together."

Vidya reaches out to hold my hand. "They will be magnificent, won't they, babe?"

I give her a weak smile. I don't like where this is going.

"I'm sorry, Vidya. I can't stay long. My friends are waiting outside. I came here to return Jacen's jacket," Elayne says.

"Tell him to throw that hideous thing away."

Before Elayne has a chance to react, I growl at Vidya first. "Vid, stop it."

Elayne's eyes dart between Vidya and me. She shifts in her seat, clearly looking for the fastest way to escape.

Vidya sits back and sips from her cup. She gives a slow smile that doesn't help ease the anxiety that's building up inside me. Then, turning to look at Elayne, she says, "I'm having a party at my place in three weeks after our exams. You should come. Bring Jacen with you."

Elayne's expression shifts from discomfort to awe within a heartbeat. "*You* want *me* to come?"

"Why not? But it's a small party, with this Covid thing happening and all. I think I'll go with a laid-back casual theme. Azraai will share the deets with Jacen."

"Thanks for the invitation, Vidya. We'll definitely come. I have to go now. Thanks again, ya?"

Vidya waves at Elayne's retreating form without taking her eyes off me. She's still wearing that same smile.

"What the fuck, Vid?" I hiss after making sure Elayne is out of earshot.

"Babe, you'll thank me later."

10

It's weird how we spent a month and a half in lockdown with no direction, followed by sporadic online courses. When the lockdown ended, we had mixed physical and online classes, and midterms had been canceled, but we were still expected to sit for our final exams. Not that I have any difficulties with the four core subjects I have for this semester except for business and economics statistics. Maybe I should have opted for an introduction to business analysis instead, as Vidya did.

The closer we get to the weekend, the more animated she becomes, but it has nothing to do with the exams. She doesn't seem to care if she passes or fails any of the subjects. The only thing on her mind right now is the party. Her guest list is close to a hundred already, and she's not supposed to have over fifty guests at a time. Apparently, she has to schedule a time slot for her invitees, excluding a few girls she's interested in and me.

Who the hell schedules slots for a party? More than that, how does one do it?

While the exams begin, I limit the time I spend with Vidya, but not because I don't want her to cheat off me. She has plenty of clueless guys volunteering to do just that. It's her incessant chatter about the party that irritates me. I'm half regretting the idea I planted in her head. The other half is torn between not wanting Jacen to show up and hoping that he does.

I have half an hour to kill before the final paper ends, and while I can leave the tutorial room, I've promised to wait for her, and she's busy copying answers off a guy to her left, two rows in front of me. I excuse myself to the toilet because there's only so much boredom I can take.

I'm not familiar with the layout of the tutorial and seminar rooms in the main block, and since I'm not in a hurry, I wander down the hallway, checking out announcements and advertisement posters on the walls. Some of them are a few years old. I can't help but chuckle when I see that the poster featuring Jacen and me is securely mounted in an acrylic frame. I wonder how many people have thought about stealing this one.

Most of the rooms are occupied. Other courses must be having their exams, too. I heard some schools have canceled their final written tests and make do with coursework and projects instead. Lucky them.

The door ahead of me opens, and, of all the people for me to stumble into, it has to be the one person I can spend several lifetimes without. "Sorry, my bad," I mumble as I back away.

The asshole looks sincerely apologetic — and somewhat cute — until he recognizes me. His face turns mean immediately. His grip on the doorknob tightens, and his entire body stiffens.

"Dude, chill," I say as softly as possible. I have no intention of making a scene in front of his entire class.

He has enough sense to close the door before replying. I'll give him that. "Don't come near me," he growls.

I hold my hands up and back away a step. "Chill, okay? I don't have Covid or anything."

"That's not what I'm worried about. I wish you and your kind of people will get Covid and die."

"*My* kind of people? I'm gay, not infectious. But your bigotry is. Or is the word too big for you to handle?"

He looks surprised at my audacity to stand up for myself, but his narrowed eyes tell me he's not about to concede or apologize.

I walk past him, but I stop long enough to whisper in his ear, "You know, usually the most homophobic people are so deep in the closet, they can't stand those who are honest about themselves."

I should have expected the punch that sends my left ear ringing. Maybe I deserve it, but fuck it hurts.

My jaw still smarts even after three days. Chewing hurts. Talking hurts. Laughing… well, I have had no reason to laugh, but I'm sure it'll hurt, too. Maybe it was the height difference or my position when the asshole punched me, but things could have been worse. The impact could have dislocated or broken my jaw; he put *that* much hatred in that single swing. I wonder if he had a punch nocked and ready to spring at me and *my kind of people*.

I had every intention of skipping Vidya's party. My swollen jaw is plain to see. I couldn't even hide it from Mak Su and the old man. At least she went into full mother hen mode. He just stood in front of his study and stared at me as I ducked into my room. Vidya doesn't buy my story of stumbling on the treadmill at the gym and knocking my jaw on the handrail, especially since I ditched her during the exam and didn't wait for her to finish as promised. She's grudgingly concerned and apologetic but insists that my presence is mandatory, even if she has to bribe RELA officers to bodily escort me to her house.

Vidya has somehow used the empty field beside her hillside mansion as a parking lot, complete with people guiding guests to maximize the space. I half expect her to provide jockey service. While her family's net worth is less than the old man's, Vidya's home is far more opulent than mine. I've been to her bungalow several times. I even crashed in her room once while waiting for her to get ready for a photoshoot we had together. Vidya's mansion has been featured in architectural and interior design magazines, but professional snapshots don't do her home justice. She's always dismissive and unhelpful when people ask her about it, but I read her dad hired a renowned Japanese architect to design the mansion from the ground up. The entire concept centers on openness and geometric balance. The four-story building is mostly off-white granite and transparent glass walls, and there's even an elevator installed. Vidya's elder brother Rohan has claimed the entire top floor as his den, and I enjoy hanging out with him for a game of pool or some impromptu jamming. Vidya's room is more modest in comparison, but still much bigger than mine.

A line has formed at the entrance. Guests are having their temperature checked, their names registered in a big book, and... their photos taken? Talk about over-the-top security. When it's my turn, I immediately understand the extra precaution.

In a yellow spaghetti strap dress that leaves little to the imagination, Vidya greets me at the door with an excited hug. To my surprise, she's wearing a mask, though it's more of a sheer face veil than an actual functional mask. "Babe, you're late. Is your face okay? It's not that swollen. I can barely see that... angry... weal. Anyway, it's a good thing you have the mask on."

"There's no such thing as being late to a party. I see what you did with the guest registration, Vid. Smart move. Genius, in fact."

Vidya grins brilliantly. "Isn't it? I can take my time going through the pictures, and if they tingle my vag, I already have their name and phone number."

"Why polaroid, though? It's unflattering."

"Because it's charming and doesn't raise suspicion. Come, everyone's out by the pool. No one's tried to jump in yet, but there may or may not be alcohol, and the day's still early."

I stop and raise both eyebrows. "Vid. Half your guests have not reached the legal drinking age. That includes us. Aren't you worried about a police raid or something?"

Vidya laughs and pats my jaw... the side that hurts, and I suspect she does it on purpose. "Babe, relax. You're not in some American teenage soap. Plus, I'm not providing the booze. I just told some guests that I wouldn't stop them if they brought their own."

"And paid for the bottles, too," I say, giving her a half-smile.

"You know me too well. It's borderline scary."

"Your parents are around?"

"They took the neighbors out for dinner."

"Smart move. Rohan?"

Vidya makes a vague wave. "I don't know. Last I saw him, he was vaping by the pool with his friends. Fair warning, though. He just broke up, so he's obnoxious about it."

"Sorry to hear that. His ex seemed like a nice girl," I say.

"Why? He's not. The idiot's ecstatic, in fact."

Mental note: don't come anywhere near Rohan.

"By the way. If you're looking for Jacen and Emilia, their slot is after eight," Vidya says.

"Elayne."

Vidya rolls her eyes, a gesture made exquisite by her glittering gold eyeshadow. "She's cute, but not enough for me to care. Go have fun. If you can't find me, don't come looking. And my room is off-limits for today. Love you, babe."

My mask brushes against her veil as I kiss her cheek. She greets other guests, and I make my way to the back. A deejay has set up his stage near the glass half wall overlooking the hill and is playing some club music that no one is dancing to. Yet. Guests are scattered everywhere around the rectangular pool, chatting, eating, and laughing. More than a handful have taken their masks off, but the only ones showing any form of body contact are couples who cannot keep their hands off each other. As far as parties go, this is a sad excuse for one, but everyone's so socially deprived, they show up anyway.

I spot a group of mutual friends and end up hanging out with them for a good hour as the sky turns golden, then red, and then the entire world desaturates as twilight settles in. All the lights come to life, giving the modern mansion a fresh look and vibe. As the sky gets darker, the deejay spins faster and raunchier songs. Some guests are dancing, which is not surprising, seeing that they have a limited time slot to get drunk and have fun at what must be the first party hosted in months.

I steal a glance at my watch. It's already half-past eight, but there are no signs of Jacen and Elayne anywhere. My phone is silent, other than I-G notifications. Vidya is also nowhere in sight. Rohan is by the far side of the pool with his friends, and he smiles and raises his glass at me every time we make eye contact. The crowds around us change, but we don't approach each other, only maintaining these friendly exchanges from afar.

Vidya appears without warning and pulls me away from our uni friends. "Guess who just arrived?" she asks as she escorts me into the house.

"The police?"

That earns me a slap on my back. "Can you not jinx the party? It's spinning out of control as it is. Some guests are overstaying their welcome, and there are definitely over fifty people right now. Also, a lot more drunk people than I can handle."

I stop and hold her arms. "You okay, Vid? Your date's a no-show or something?"

"She's around. *She* I don't mind getting tipsy. Playing host is taking more time and effort than I expected, is all."

"You want me to shut down the party? I'll gladly do it."

Vidya pats my chest and gives me an overly innocent grin. "And turn away the one person you've been looking out for the whole time you were out there?"

"What..."

"Babe. Just because you didn't see me doesn't mean I wasn't keeping an eye on you. Now, where are they? I swear I left them here a moment ago...."

It's hard not to notice Jacen in a gray hoodie that clings to his shoulders, arms, and chest, standing beside the black leather sofa in the living room. He's chatting with a couple of guys from the uni. He's wearing a black mask, but his eyebrows are expressive enough.

Just as I'm about to greet Jacen, I notice a more petite figure sitting on the armrest, chatting animatedly with the same guys. Elayne. And she's wearing *his* jacket over her floral blouse.

What's with her and his jacket, anyway? And in *this* weather, too.

Vidya leans in and whispers, "Babe, jealousy is a good look on you. You should wear it more often."

"I'm not jealous."

"Sure. Tell yourself that."

Before I can turn away, Jacen spots me and waves. Vidya nudges me forward before abandoning me to chat with another guest. Left with no choice, I sigh and walk toward him. We meet halfway.

Jacen lowers his mask and smiles at me with his entire face. "Looking good, Azraai with a double A."

I make a show of dusting my loose-fitting batik shirt and khaki slacks. "Everything looks good on me." Without thinking, I glance at Elayne. More specifically, at the jacket she's wearing.

"Been here long?" Jacen asks.

"I'm about to leave, actually," I say, and I mean it.

"But we just got here. And to be honest, I'm not used to this."

I raise an eyebrow. "Partying? You sure?"

"No. This social scene. It's way above my bracket, and everything's a bit… overwhelming."

"They have good booze by the pool. Maybe that'll help take off the edge a little. Does Elayne drink?"

Jacen shrugs. "I have no idea. But thanks for the tip. Don't go back yet? Hang around for a while?"

I have to learn to say no to him. Maybe after tonight. "Go. Mingle around. I wanna find something to eat in the kitchen."

Jacen pumps his fists in victory. "Cool. Elayne wants to check out this freaking immense place. The good stuff's by the pool, right? Which way?"

I point in the general direction of the backyard and then make my way to the kitchen. The buffet spread is outside, but extra food and dishes that some guests brought are stacked on the granite island in the middle of the dry kitchen. I'm not alone in thinking of raiding the kitchen, though. One of our classmates has already claimed a high stool. I sit next to her, and we end up sampling most of the food. I didn't realize I was this hungry.

66

Jacen doesn't show up even after I'm done stuffing myself. I leave the small group who have joined us in helping ourselves to the food on the island and look around for Jacen. I spot the unmistakable oversized faux leather jacket and Elayne's coppery hair near a dimly lit corner of the zen garden. She stands on her toes, with her back toward me and her head tilted upward. Jacen, his hands on her waist, leans down to meet her in a kiss.

There aren't many things I regret in life. Seeing them locking lips tops that list.

Even with my eyes closed, I can still see them kissing.

My vision turns red, and my heart thumps in my head. The worst part is that I don't know why I'm reacting this way. I back a step, then two, and instinct takes over the wheel. My feet take me from the crowded backyard and pool, past the dining areas and living rooms, and down a quiet corridor that ends with an elevator. A handwritten DO NOT ENTER on a piece of A4 paper has been pasted on the glass-and-steel door, but I ignore it and tap the button repeatedly until the car comes down and the door slides open.

When the door on the top floor opens, I stumble out. The entire floor is dimly lit, with its primary source of illumination a huge-ass wall-mounted TV playing a car chase scene on mute. The plush three-seater sofa in front of the TV is empty. While the rest of the house is granite and glass, Rohan's den is covered almost entirely with wood, from the floor to the walls to the pillars that double as book- and display shelves.

"Didn't you see the... Azraai, is that you?"

Rohan stands at the doorway of his room in nothing but what looks like a pair of satin lounge pants. Even in the low light, his form is perfectly illuminated. He has the physique of an Olympic swimmer, except that he has a wealth of chest hair that tracks down his navel. The treasure trail disappears behind the band of his pants. I still wonder why Rohan doesn't do modeling or venture into the entertainment business, although I've seen him rocking a full business suit before.

"Sorry, Rohan. Didn't know you were up here. I just needed to —"

He traps me with his gaze, just like how Vidya does. Seriously, did they grow up locked in staring contests every day? "Escape from the crowd? Or someone in particular?" he asks.

Backing away toward the elevator, I say, "I didn't mean to intrude. I'll leave you to it."

Rohan chuckles as he picks up a cylindrical glass from the counter just outside his room. He points at the sofa and makes his way there. "Absurdité. Ma maison est ta maison. Come, join me. Single malt whiskey? Or are you a bourbon guy? Champagne?"

I wonder if his French works on girls every time. Despite myself, I head to the sofa. I sit at one end, and he plops down at the other. His muscles *ripple* with each movement. I'm not surprised if he has less than eight percent body fat. My eyes inadvertently follow his treasure trail and settle on the outline of his dick under the maroon lounge pants. It can't be *that* soft to be that impressive, surely. I tear my gaze away and meet his eyes. His smirk tells me he knows what I was looking at. Shit.

I clear my throat. "Thanks. I don't drink. I feel like getting so drunk I'd forget everything in the morning, though."

Rohan turns the glass in his hands before taking a sip. "Not to be the snake or anything, but why don't you? What's there to lose?"

I huff a sigh and slump deeper against the plush sofa. "I keep asking myself that question every time someone offers me a drink. There are still some lines that I don't want to cross. Yet."

Rohan shifts obliquely to face me. He's fairer than Vidya, which makes the contrast from his black facial and chest hair even more alluring. He could seriously be a Hindustani movie star. "What about the lines you cross, Azraai?" he asks.

Certainly not this. He's Vidya's brother, for fuck's sake.

Then again, Vidya never mentioned that Rohan was off-limits. I'm fucking horny right now, but I didn't just run away from one straight guy to get tangled with another, however hot and inviting he may be.

"Vid told me you just broke up with your girlfriend. That's rough. Sorry," I say.

"Why? I'm not." When did he get closer?

"I'm sure you'll find another girl soon. You didn't find anyone interesting at the party?"

Rohan's lazy one-sided grin cuts a deep dimple onto his cheek. "Maybe I have found someone. Maybe that someone found me."

No point feigning cluelessness. "But you like girls," I say, edging a millimeter away.

"Girls. Guys. Why put labels on and limit myself? Beautiful people attract me. And Azraai, tu es magnifique."

Rohan puts his empty glass on the coffee table and leans so close he's on top of me. I'm heady with the scent of his wood-and-earth cologne mixed with the whiskey on his breath. There's a gradually narrowing space between his upper body and mine, but his crotch is already pressed against my thigh. I can feel him hardening. Not like an excited puppy, but a predator stretching to warm up for the hunt.

I press my hands against his chest. Though surprisingly thick and coarse, the trimmed hair is collectively soft as his satin pants. His pecs tense against my palms. "Rohan, you're drunk," I say.

"What if I am? Where both consenting adults," he whispers, a few octaves lower than his usual voice. He takes his time to utter each syllable.

"I don't remember consenting," I whisper back, even though we're alone in his den.

"But your body is already saying yes," he says, smirking. He knows I'm getting hard, too. Fuck.

I find it harder to form words, even in my head. "Rohan…"

He bites his lip and lowers his upper body until we're almost touching. The hairs on his body rise in static to bridge the gap. He leans in for a kiss, but I turn away at the very last moment. Undeterred, Rohan kisses my jawbone instead.

The part that still hurts.

The pain is as effective as plunging myself into icy water to dispel the haze in my mind. I push his chest again, this time with more conviction. "Rohan, stop. This is not a good idea, tempting though, as it is."

Rohan plants a quick kiss on my nose tip before pushing himself away. Still smiling, he says, "Is it because I'm Vidya's brother?"

I slowly adjust myself to my original sitting position. I don't bother hiding my hard-on because, what's the point, really? "That, and you're drunk and just broke up." And then I add, almost under my breath, "And I'm a mess right now."

Rohan reaches for his flat, compact vape from the coffee table and takes a huff. He offers it to me, and I take a long drag until my throat and lungs burn. While the flavor I inhale is melon, the smoke leaves an acrid taste on my tongue when I exhale.

"You want to talk about it?" Rohan asks.

"No. But I need to leave, though. It's getting late. I don't want to be caught in a random roadblock."

Rohan reaches over and squeezes my shoulder. "My floor is always open for you if you feel like talking. Or if you want to pick up where we left off."

"Thanks, Rohan. And… sorry."

Rohan exhales white smoke from his nostrils and mouth. "Non, mon ami. Few people can resist my charm, so I take this as a challenge. Or not, up to you."

"It's the French," I say, grinning at him.

"Je sais."

Rohan sends me off to the elevator door. He's only a breath shorter, so he doesn't have to reach up when he gives me a one-armed hug. I pat his smooth back.

"Take care, Azraai. And you know where to find me if you want to have a little fun," Rohan says as the door slides closed.

I shake my head and give him a wave-salute. Downstairs, the party is winding down, and the guests are leaving. I can't find Vidya anywhere, so I text her I'm leaving, too.

Just outside the main gate, I spot a broad-backed figure with his gray hoodie draped over his head, sitting on the curb facing the road. I walk closer and call out, "Jacen?"

Jacen whips around and almost loses his balance. His cheeks are flushed and his eyes are bloodshot. "Azraai? I thought you left."

I sit beside him. He reeks of alcohol. "What are you doing here? Where's Elayne?"

"She left. Took a Grab home."

"You didn't drive here?"

Jacen shakes his head. "I don't have a car. I left my wallet in my jacket."

I can't help by smile. "Let me guess. She has the jacket."

Jacen nods with his entire body. "Correct."

"Why not call one for yourself?"

He fishes out his phone from his back pocket and shows me the dark screen. "Battery's dead."

Sighing, I stand up, dust the seat of my pants, and then offer him my hand. "Good thing your personal Grab driver is here, then. Come on. I'll send you home."

Jacen blinks at my hand a few times before taking it. I haul him up and lock his arm with mine to prevent him from swaying too much as we walk to my car.

"How much did you drink?" I ask.

"Before or after Elayne left?"

"You didn't do those jello shots, did you?"

"I thought they were just jello."

I chuckle and keep my peace. The last thing a drunk person needs is an interrogation. I lead him to the car, secure him in the passenger seat, and reach close to buckle the seatbelt for him. He doesn't resist or push me away.

"Give me your address before you fall asleep," I say once I've started the engine and connected my phone to the car.

Just as I'm about to reverse from the parking spot, my phone chirps. Vidya's personal WhatsApp sound.

```
[Vidya] : babe where r u I need u
```

I stare at the text, then at Jacen, who's adjusting himself in his seat to get more comfortable with his eyes closed. His cheeks and ears are red. He opens his eyes briefly to look at me and then smiles.

I drop the phone into the cup holder and grip the steering wheel. I'm sure Vidya will forgive me later.

11

Fuck it. I'm a terrible friend.

I make a complete circle at the roundabout in front of the main entrance of the gated community before turning back. The makeshift parking lot is mostly empty, and I drive past it and head straight to Vidya's driveway. A van is parked near the front doors, and disheveled, tired-looking caterers are loading trays and leftover food into the van.

I park beside Vidya's gray Mini. Jacen is halfway between awake and asleep. I adjust the air-conditioning to a comfortable 23 Celsius and tap on Jacen's arm to get his attention.

"Push the seat back and get some rest. I need to check in on Vidya for a bit. I won't be long, I hope. Try not to barf inside the car," I say.

"You're a good friend," he mumbles, and a strong whiff of alcohol fills the car. How many shots did he take? I consider switching off the engine and letting down the windows, but having Jacen drown in his own sweat will be too much punishment. For my car.

"No, I'm not," I say as I shut the door.

A few guests are still hanging out and chatting, but the maids are already busy picking up trash and discarded tableware. I rush past them and climb the stairs two steps at a go. Vidya's room is on the second floor. I knock on the door, but when no one answers, I let myself in. I switch on the lights and find discarded clothes and underwear on the carpeted floor. The king-sized bed is a total mess. At least someone had a good time tonight.

"Vid?"

"In here," comes a muffled reply behind partially opened sliding doors.

Vidya's walk-in closet is nothing short of impressive. While her room is almost a typical luxury designer space, the closet is something else together. Shelves and racks line the two walls, and the hanging clothes are not just coordinated in color but also in length. Three columns of floor-to-ceiling display shelves are dedicated to her designer shoes alone, and on the opposite wall are her handbags, clutches, and purses. Some articles are from this year's Fashion Week lines. The island in the middle of the room houses her countless accessories. Despite the sheer amount of clothing, the closet doesn't feel or look cluttered, probably because it's almost as big as her main room.

"Vid, where are you?"

"At the back."

Now that Vidya's voice is clearer, I can catch the cracks and the sobs that follow. I find her slumped against the mirror that occupies the entire far wall. She's in an oversized T-shirt with holes that I'm sure were designed that way. Her hair and makeup are in a worse condition than her bed. I squat in front of her and hold her hand.

"Hey, what happened?"

Vidya's sobs get more intense, and I can barely understand her when she blurts out, "She called me an experiment."

I settle down beside her and clasp her hand close to my chest. We stay this way as she cries, and I keep still when she buries her face in my shoulder. I don't need to ask for details because I get her completely. This is the one reason I hate getting tangled with straight people. They're a mess, but they leave an even bigger shitstorm when they discard us.

"I should have known better," she finally says between an odd mixture of sobs and hiccups. Her tears continue to soak my shirt.

"Vid…"

"I should have seen the signs. This is all my fault."

"Vid, no."

"Jesus Christ, I should have seen it coming. But she was so —"

"Hot?" I ask with a low chuckle.

Vidya gives a half-hearted laugh. That's a good sign. "So hot."

We stay quiet for a few more minutes before I ask, "Judging from the situation outside, I assume the experiment was fruitful, at least?"

Which earns me a tickling jab on my side. "I bet I was the first

73

orgasm she didn't need to fake. But afterward, she told me she still preferred a real dick."

"*She's* the real dick," I say.

"The biggest."

"As if you've seen enough dicks to compare sizes. Have you seen any, for that matter?"

Vidya jabs me again, but this time she laughs in earnest. She rests her head on my wet shoulder and sighs. "Look at us. Two queers in a *literal* closet."

I make a show of looking around and admiring the view. "As far as closets go, I don't mind living in this one. I'm impressed, Vid. No wonder you take so long to get ready."

"This is my zen garden. Speaking of, is the party over? Please tell me Rohan is at least a half-decent co-host."

I shake my head & lean back even more. "He's in his den."

"I knew it. I have to do everything myself. Did he tell you he was abandoning his responsibility?"

"I... ah... met him upstairs."

Vidya immediately sits up and locks me with her eyes. "You went upstairs? Did he take advantage of you?"

I squirm but cannot escape her stare. I really need to take notes from these two siblings. "We... kinda had... a... moment?"

"He works fast," she says, her face contemplative.

I blink stupidly at her. "You're okay with it?"

Vidya gives a dismissive shrug. "It's not like he has to compete with me to get in your pants."

"Fair point."

"He's had his eyes on you since the first time he saw you here," she says.

"You know he's bisexual?"

Vidya rolls her eyes, but with her mascara and makeup a disaster of abstract art on her face, the effect isn't the same. "Try pan. He screws anything that moves. He's the reason I'm able to accept myself this easily."

"Your parents are on board?"

"Other than the cringe-worthy safe sex talk? Yeah, they're cool."

Accepting who you are is one thing, but being open about it with your *living* family is something I don't dare imagine. I'm already a disappointment in the old man's eyes, but I don't think I'll ever be ready to break Mak Su's heart this way. I guess I'm still in a closet of my making.

"So is this thing with Rohan happening, or are you still hung up on your own hot, straight experiment?"

Jacen. Shit. I forgot about him. "Vid, I have a confession to make. Said hot experiment is waiting in my car."

Vidya's eyes, messy as they are, light up. "Babe. Do tell."

"He's drunk and sleeping it off. I hope."

"Even better. Are *you* going to take advantage of him?"

It's my turn to poke at Vidya's side. "Don't be gross. I'm just sending him home."

"What are you doing here, then? Jesus Christ, do you want him to die from monoxide poisoning or something?"

"I wanna make sure you're okay first," I say.

Vidya wipes her face with her T-shirt and then stares at the multi-colored smudge in horror. "Babe. You *did not* tell me about my face situation."

"You just made it worse."

Vidya turns to look at herself in the mirror and then grabs her phone and poses for a selfie. When she sees my raised eyebrows, she shrugs and says, "Maybe I'll post it on Insta or Fanhouse later and use an artsy hashtag or something. Just go. I'll be fine. I just need to nurse my bruised ego and hide in here a bit more. Maybe overnight."

"Do you need some wet wipes or makeup remover? I can grab whatever you want from your bathroom."

Vidya shakes her head.

"What about getting rid of any incriminatory evidence from your room?"

"Like you know what to look for."

I scrunch my face. "I don't even want to find out."

I envelop Vidya in an awkward bear hug and then leave her to adjust the smudges on her face before taking more selfies. Like I said, her social media life is strictly curated, even the uglier sides that she deems worth sharing.

By the time I come down, all the guests have left, and the maids have moved on to the kitchen to scrub it clean. The living areas are already back to their pre-party spotless condition. Outside, the caterers are loading the last of their stuff. Jacen is asleep, his head resting against the window. His snore is light, almost like a purr.

It's a good thing the way to his house is relatively empty and free from roadblocks. The car reeks of alcohol. If we were stopped, I wouldn't know how to explain myself to the police.

Initially, I thought the navigation led me to the wrong place. I stop my car by the roadside of the four high-rise flat buildings on the outskirts of Ampang, near the Hulu Langat border. The parking lots are packed with double-parked cars and motorcycles, and the red paint of all four buildings illuminated by the streetlights has peeled away in most places, showing stained white underpaint and black mold. From the looks of it, there must be at least a hundred families living in one building alone.

I pat Jacen's shoulder until he wakes up, and after several moments' worth of disorientation, he looks around before settling his unfocused gaze on me. "We're here. Thanks for the ride," he says.

So we're *not* at the wrong place after all. I switch off the engine and unbuckle my seatbelt.

"It's okay, Azraai. I can make it home on my own."

With my hands still on the seatbelt, I look at Jacen and say, "Can you even stand straight right now?"

Luckily, I'm already outside his door when he's gathered himself enough to exit the car. Jacen stands up, wobbles, and then lands at the side edge of the seat. He accepts my offer to help him to the elevator with a slow, careful nod. I lock his arm with mine and let him lean on me as we make our way to his block. Stray cats pitter-patter toward us, their wails more than making up for their padded steps. Most of them look well-fed, and more than a few are plainly pregnant, but their furs are grimy and their ears are crusted with infection. I'm certain that each of them hosts entire villages of fleas. The cats follow us and beg for food, but they eventually lose interest when I have nothing to offer. Mounds of fly- and ant-infested garbage bags and loose trash occupy the small grassy space beside Jacen's block. I do my best to avoid puddles on the cement floor; it hasn't rained, so I have no idea what the collections are. The breeze carries a stale stench of some dead animal. Maybe one of the cats, or their prey. The entire place screams of humanity pressed into a tight space.

When we reach the elevator, traffic cones stand in front of both doors, and a massive OUT OF SERVICE sign hangs on the wall in between, covering the buttons.

I heft Jacen straighter and point at the sign. "Which floor are you? Looks like we have to use the stairs."

"Ninth."

I look up at the stairwell between the two arms of the flat block. Not only is it narrow and dimly lit, on at least two floors it gets dark altogether. I hoist Jacen closer, sling his arm across my shoulder, and wrap my arm around his waist. I hook my thumb on the belt loop of his jeans. Jacen swings his head toward me, but must have regretted the sudden movement. He closes his eyes for several moments before signaling me to walk.

Navigating the first three floors proves to be a challenge because Jacen sways too much, and I have to put my free hand on the wall whenever we reach a landing between floors to keep my balance. It takes supreme effort not to dwell on how dirty the surfaces I'm forced to touch are. Also, some residents have somehow seen fit to line the stairs with potted plants that take up at least a quarter of the space.

By the time we reach the fourth floor, the back of my shirt is already drenched. The mixture of sweat, alcohol breath, and trash discarded in the stairwell is not something my nose can take, but I trudge on, one step at a time. To Jacen's credit, he does his best not to make this any more difficult. The block numbers painted on the sidewall are the only sign that we're making any progress. Of all the situations I conjured up where I'm this close to Jacen, I never imagined this.

When we swing around the landing between the seventh and eighth floors, Jacen grasps the banister and refuses to take another step. "Azraai, wait. We're going too fast. My head's spinning."

Here I'm thinking we're already taking *hours* to reach his floor. I don't argue with him, though. I need to catch my breath, too. "We're almost there," I say.

Shaking his head, Jacen says, "I know, but—"

Jacen loses his balance, and without thinking, I pull him into a tight hug. He gasps for air before ending up vomiting. His barf hits the wall and splashes on my already slurping back. Some of it lands on my shoulder as it escapes his mouth. How much did he drink? And what the fuck did he eat? I gag and bite the nearest thing I can find, which is his hoodie, to stop myself from adding my barf to the thick pool cascading down the stairs. This is *definitely not* how I imagined the night would end.

Doing my best not to gag further at the overwhelming stench, I lead him to the ninth floor. Jacen seems to have sobered up after vomiting because his steps are lighter and surer. We walk along the open-air corridor of his floor, past shoes and flip-flops scattered in front of each unit's door, past racks and potted plants that make the walkway cluttered and narrow, and stop in front of his unit near the end. The windows are dark, and the entire house is quiet. Jacen retrieves his set of keys from his pocket and carefully unlocks the grille and wooden door, barely making a sound.

"Wait here. I'll get you a fresh T-shirt," he says.

"Can I come in and wash up first? I can't stand my own smell right now."

Jacen eases the door open to a slit and peers in before turning back to face me. "My brother and I sleep in the living room, and he's a light sleeper. He doesn't deal with strangers that well, and I don't want the entire block to wake up. Wait here, okay?"

Left with no choice, I lean on the rusty railing and study the opposite block. Everything is so packed together, that the only breathing space is probably inside the individual units. I wonder how many rooms they have if Jacen and his brother sleep outside. Or maybe that's just an excuse not to let me in.

Before I can dwell on the thought any further, the door opens long enough for Jacen to step out. He has freshened up and his hair is dripping. He hands me a black collared T. I unbutton my shirt, but he stops me by resting his hand on mine. When I look down, he pulls his hand back immediately.

"What are you doing?" he whispers.

"What does it look like? I need to get out of this shirt. Like, now."

"Right here?"

I throw him an accusing look that I hope he understands. "Or you can let me in."

"Sorry, Azraai. My brother almost woke up when I entered just now. I figured you were going to change in the car."

"Not gonna happen," I say, and take off my shirt. The collared T fits me well. I point at the Starbucks logo on the chest.

Jacen shrugs, half smiling. "Sorry. That's the newest clean top I have. I've only worn it twice, I promise."

"I don't care. I'm gonna keep it," I say.

Jacen chuckles and shakes his head. Wet strands of hair fall and cover his eyes.

Pointing at the shirt hanging on the railing, I ask, "Where can I throw that?"

"Why would you want to do that? It's silk batik, right? Must be expensive."

"There's makeup, tears, sweat, and… oh, wait… barf everywhere. No way I'm going to wear it again."

"Let me wash it for you. It's the least I can do."

"Doesn't mean I'll wear it," I say. Then, almost playfully, I add, "Unless you prove to me the shirt is still usable."

Jacen grabs the shirt before I can reach for it. We end up standing so close; he inhales the air I exhale. My breaths become heavier, slower. His, too.

Before I can stop myself, I reach up and comb the hair away from his eyes. A warm sensation expands in waves where my skin meets his.

"Azraai…"

"Hmm…"

"I… Elayne."

I nod, once. Our nose tips brush. The warm wave spreads throughout my face.

"Azraai…"

"Hmm…"

"I like… I like girls."

Whatever fumes the moment has me drunk on, Jacen's words sober me up real good. I take a step back, then another, but the railing prevents me from backing any farther. "Yeah, I need to check in on Vidya. She was still in an awful shape when I left."

"Azraai—"

"Sleep it off and don't get this drunk again, okay? Thanks for the shirt. I'll see you… when I see you, I guess."

"Azraai, please."

I ignore the plea and anguish in Jacen's voice. Maybe it's pity. And guilt. I should not have done this in the first place. I should have seen this coming.

Not caring what I touch and step on, I race down the stairwell at a breakneck speed. I can smell him every time I take a deep breath because this fucking shirt has his fucking scent.

I feel like taking off the top and discarding it, but not here.

I need to be anywhere but here.

12

The entire uni feels deserted. The semester has more or less ended, but the overachiever in me took on an additional elective course that no one else in my class has registered for: Basic Mandarin for Business. I figured a formal credit would help me get farther in this field. Besides, it's fun to have people talking in Mandarin in front of me, assuming I don't understand a single word.

A whopping total of six students from different Schools are sitting for the exam this semester. For the oral assessment, we're required to sit in booths with an empty seat in between, listen to the instructions over noise-canceling headphones, and then record our replies on the laptops. The exam is ninety minutes long, and I barely make it in time. By the time I finish, my mouth and jaw are aching from trying to enunciate the words as perfectly as I can.

I go to the basement toilet before leaving, but not because I'm looking for some action. I'm just more comfortable shitting in total privacy. There are better places I can go to, people I can hook up with if I wanted to get blown.

Last Saturday night has left me horny and frustrated, but above all, angry at myself. I advised Vidya not to blame herself for being an experiment, but here I am, wallowing in self-pity. Fuck my life.

The toilet door opens as I wash my hands at the sink after I'm done with my business. Of all the people to cross my path today, why must it be the asshole? I ignore him, but I cannot ignore his reflection looking straight at me.

"If you plan on punching me again, can we do it some other day?

I'm not in the mood today," I say.

I wipe my hands on my jeans, and head for the exit, but he blocks my path. I sidestep. He stands wider.

"Faggot," he says—no, spits with clear venom.

That's it. Fuck this shit. I ram against him, push him to the wall, and grab his crotch. Fuck. He's already hard. I grab his hand with my free one and force him to hold my crotch. He struggles for a bit, but when I massage his dick over his jeans, he lets out a soft whimper and his eyes roll back until the whites show.

Not letting go of my grip, I guide him to one stall. I nibble his earlobe before pushing him down to the seat. He spreads his legs, and I kneel in front of him. I close the door, but I don't bother locking it. It swings back ajar and stops only when it hits my back.

"Wait. Someone can see us," he says between ragged breaths.

"Just shut up. No one comes here."

I unzip his jeans and he pushes them along with his checkered boxers halfway down his thighs. His hard dick slaps against his body when he releases it from its confinement. He has a husband dick, average in length, but the girth is almost impressive. It's a shame he doesn't shave or trim. His entire body shudders when I circle my hand around his dick and start pumping. He holds my head and guides me down. A moan escapes his lips as I wrap mine around his throbbing mushroom head.

Huh. I guess my theory about him being so deep in the closet that he's resentful is correct after all.

I have to admit; he has impressive control. He intermittently stops me, tenses up for a few seconds, and then guides my head back up and down his shaft. I gobble him up to the base of his dick, which is my forte, and he shudders even more. His musk is thick, heady. He's lasting longer than most of my casual encounters, but I don't care.

When he is close to orgasm, I pull my head back, but he stops me midway and explodes in my mouth. His warmth fills me up fast, and I gag and cough to prevent myself from swallowing any of it. I slam my hands on the stall walls and struggle to free myself, but his grip is strong. He spasms and twitches with me still gagging and spitting, his dick in my mouth, until he is spent.

When he finally releases his grip, I scramble away, slamming the door shut against my back. I gag and spit and damn near vomit out my breakfast, but his taste is still thick in my mouth.

"What. The. Fuck?!"

He leans back and smiles at me. He looks sleepy, almost. Before he can answer, though, a phone comes to life outside the stall. The sudden ringtone coming from the sink area sounds like a game theme song. Super Smash Bros.

The asshole mirrors my wide-eyed horror.

As abruptly as the sound invaded the toilet, it stops. The sounds of rubber soles on the tiled floor precede the swinging of the main door. I scurry up and rush to the exit, but whoever was with us in the toilet is now gone. I walk back to the stall to see the asshole stuffing his semi-hard, glistening wet dick back in his pants.

"You think they saw us?" he asks.

"Even if they didn't, they could have heard me gagging. What the fuck was that? Not cool at all," I say, using my full height to block his only exit.

"What, you want me to suck your cock? No way, faggot," he says, and pushes me away.

I ball my trembling fist and punch the stall door so hard the top hinge comes loose. He washes his hands and sniggers at me before leaving as if nothing happened. This is not how things usually go. *I hold the power, not the other way 'round.*

I gargle and cough and spit until my throat is raw, but I can still taste the lingering phantom of his filth on my tongue. I brush it using my teeth and fingernails to get rid of all traces of the fucking asshole.

I will not fall apart. I refuse to succumb. Before leaving the toilet, I gargle and splash water on my face.

I cross the empty field in the blazing heat to get to my car faster. The parking lot is nearly empty. When I reach for the doorknob, the unlock button somehow refuses to work. My hands are shaking, and I drop my keys as soon as I take them out of the pocket. My eyesight is blurry from sweat dripping down my scalp and forehead. Or are they errant tears? I don't want to know.

A group of guys surrounds me when I retrieve my keys, led by the asshole.

Sneering at me, he says, "We know what you did in the toilet, faggot."

I seldom find myself disoriented and confused as much as I am right now. I raise both eyebrows at him. "What are you talking about?"

"Someone shared a video of you on your knees giving a blowjob. Did you enjoy it, huh, faggot?"

"Someone recorded what we—"

Before I can finish talking, he punches me squarely in my stomach, knocking the air out of my lungs. His friends must have taken it as a signal to start ganking me. I crumple to the burning Tarmac and ball myself as they kick and punch me over and over again.

There's no point fighting back. I curl on the ground, half of me punished by the heat, and the other half becoming the receiving end of thumps and whacks. I force myself back to the eerie stillness right after the gray van hit my mom's car before my entire world was uprooted. The hits keep coming, and my entire body screams in pain, but in that stillness, they cannot break me.

Not when I'm already shattered.

When the attacks finally cease, the asshole squats over my head and leans down to whisper, "Tell anyone and you're dead."

I finally allow myself to breathe when I hear the footsteps receding. Just as I'm about to lose consciousness, I hear a ringtone.

Super Smash Bros.

I don't want to wake up. Waking up hurts.

I feel for the button that releases morphine into my bloodstream. It helps with the pain, but more importantly, it numbs my anguish. I drift in and out of sleep every time I press the button, and while I can barely recall the weird drug-induced dreams, I remember feeling safe and warm in these dreamscapes.

Dreamscapes. Dreams that help me escape.

I giggle at this notion. The right side of my face smarts. It hurts, but the wordplay is funnier. I think.

Someone grasps my left hand. My bones hurt when they move.

The knee bone's connected to the… thigh bone.

The thigh bone's connected to the… hip bone.

The hip bone…

"Welcome back, babe. You got us worried."

Was the song just in my head or was I actually singing? I know that rich voice. Vidya's. I peel my eyes open. Focusing is another issue altogether. What's the hip bone connected to, again? "Who are you?" I ask.

Vidya clasps my hand to her lips. They're trembling.

I giggle again. This time, even my chest hurts. "Joking, Vid."

Vidya jabs my side, which brings a whole new level of agony. She panics when I tense up. "Jesus Christ. Babe, I'm so sorry."

I ride the wave until it subsides to the background. The pain doesn't completely go away, and my mind's too muddled for me to return to that still moment.

"Does it hurt? Did I break anything?" Vidya's voice is heavy with concern.

"Help me up, Vid."

She presses several buttons at the side of the bed before getting the correct one. I grit my teeth and control my breath, not wanting Vidya to see how excruciating each movement is. She raises the back halfway upright and adjusts my pillow to a more comfortable position.

"How bad is it?" I ask once the new wave of pain settles down.

"Several cracked ribs and bruises all over your body. But babe, your face...."

Panicking, I touch my face. Big mistake. "Ow. What's the damage?"

"Your right cheek is singed, and you have a cut upper lip. But the doctor said there wouldn't be any permanent scars. Except maybe your lip. No promises, he said. You protected your face, babe. I'm so proud of you. By the way, guess who's here."

"Mak Su?"

Vidya gives a wide smile. "Technically, she's here. She went down to pray. She'll be ecstatic to see you awake. Guess again."

I want to say the old man, but that feels too far-fetched. When I carefully shrug, hoping to minimize the pain, Vidya points at the other side of the room with her chin. Someone is slumped on the two-seater sofa, asleep.

Jacen.

"He's been here since yesterday. He's still wearing the same clothes," she says.

"Why?"

Vidya looks at me as though I'm the dumbest guy in the world. "He didn't bring spare clothes? Did you get kicked in the head?"

"I mean, why is he here?"

"Ask me why I'm here instead of shopping for new shoes. Come on, ask me."

I'm not sure if Vidya's being sarcastic or she's taken offense or something. The morphine is doing a number on me. "Because you love me, and you're worried about me?"

"Close enough. I'm more concerned about your face and future as a fellow model. So why do you think he's here? What happened, anyway? Were you mugged? Did you piss off someone's boyfriend? Or girlfriend?"

"Slow down, Vid. My head hurts."

The sofa creaks as Jacen stretches his long legs and arms. He gives a big yawn, stretches once more, and then rises from his seat. "This first-class ward is way more comfortable than my house. Feels bigger, too. Wait. Azraai, you're awake," he says.

Jacen doesn't approach me. Instead, he stands there awkwardly. I would act the same way if I were in his shoes. Worse, I don't think I'd show up at all, much less spend the night. Why is he here?

"Go freshen up, Quan. You look worse than Azraai," Vidya says.

Jacen wipes the corners of his mouth. "I'm good, Vidya. Thanks."

I look at Vidya, then at Jacen, and back at Vidya. "You guys know each other?"

Vidya rolls her eyes. "What did you think we did while you were in Happy Land? Sit here, teary-eyed, praying that you'd wake up?"

Jacen clears his throat. "You were doing just that when I arrived yesterday," he says, his voice soft.

"And I'd appreciate it if you didn't tell anyone about it, Quan. I have a reputation to uphold," she says.

"Sorry. How are you feeling, Azraai? What happened? The parking lot doesn't have any CCTV, so the uni doesn't have an answer. Good thing the security guard was making his rounds when he found you," he says.

"And who informed you guys?" I ask.

Jacen says, "Vidya" and Vidya says, "Mak Su" simultaneously.

"You have his number?" I ask.

"Party guest list? Hello?"

Well, she got me there. Why she would think of calling him is another matter. I guess if I had told her what happened that night, he wouldn't be here. I'm still unsure if I should thank Vidya or not.

When the door opens, I prepare myself to be smothered by Mak Su's teary embrace. But it's not Mak Su who storms in. It's the old man, followed closely by his mousey personal assistant. I steel myself for an interrogation.

"Azraai. You have company. Good to see you again, Vidya. I hope your parents and brother are well. And you are…?" the old man asks, looking at Jacen, whose eyes are darting between Vidya and me.

"Sir, I'm Jacen, Azraai's… friend," he says.

I catch his hesitation. Are we even friends? Or acquaintances? Perhaps an experiment gone wrong. I guess under normal circumstances, he'd approach the old man for a handshake. But these are not normal times.

The old man nods. "Yes. Suzita told me you stayed the night. Thank you, young man. Where is she, anyway?"

"Mak Su went down for a bit. Dzuhur prayer, is it?" Vidya says.

"How are you feeling? Is the room comfortable enough? I was told the view is great."

Trust the old man to reach for small talk. I look at the window. The heavy metallic red drapes are drawn to the sides, but the white ones cover the entire floor-to-ceiling window panels. So I can't tell if the view is great or not. I can almost see a white elephant... or maybe a hippo... lumbering to the center of the room and settling down, thinking itself invisible. That's how awkward the situation is. Where is Mak Su when I need her?

Vidya's phone chimes, and she seems to play a video because she quickly turns the volume all the way down. She displays a gamut of expressions that settles with... embarrassment? Pity? Understanding? She passes me her phone, and Jacen makes a giant beeline to my side, discarding his earlier reservation. The old man's assistant's phone also dings, but he doesn't reduce the volume. I don't need three guesses to know that we're watching the same thing.

Someone shared a four-minute video on the AzraAiNi group chat. The video is shaky, and the quality is terrible, as expected of a compressed clip shared via WhatsApp. It shows a zoomed-in view of a partially open toilet stall and the back of a chestnut-haired guy kneeling on the floor, his head bobbing up and down, accompanied by moans and slurping sounds. As for the other guy, only his spread legs and white tennis shoes are visible. This goes on for a few minutes until the kneeling guy gags and coughs and slams the stall walls with both hands, spasming as he struggles to get away. The clip ends with the guy backing away until the door bangs shut, and he yells, "What the fuck?". Then the view revolves uncontrollably before blacking out.

I yelled that. Granted, the voice is more guttural, but there's no escaping this one. Dato' Hanis's stern warning rings unnaturally clear in my head.

I steal a glance at the old man. His face is grim. I don't need to see the pity on Jacen's face. I didn't want him to find out who I really am. Not this way.

The elephant has grown in size. I can feel its weight pressing on me. I can't breathe.

"Was this you?" the old man asks without looking up from his assistant's phone.

How do I answer him? In front of everyone? To make things worse, Mak Su walks in and rushes to my side when she sees me sitting up. She's crying, babbling about how she just prayed for me to regain consciousness.

Jacen clears his throat. "That toilet can be anywhere. And many people dye their hair that color. You can't see the faces at all. And Azraai doesn't sound like that," he says with all the conviction I don't have.

The old man nods. "Yes, you're right." Then, to his assistant, he says, "Trace the original sender and shut this down. Kill the clip and stop it from getting distributed farther if possible. Prepare a statement to deny Azraai's involvement if it comes to that. Also, the university owes us more than an apology for letting my son get mugged in their compound. Make sure they do everything in their power to stop any rumors from spreading."

"I wasn't mugged—"

He reaches for my wallet in the side drawer and shows me the empty banknote compartment. "Yes, you were, son. You probably had a concussion."

"I didn't bring any—"

"They took your cash. How much was inside? Four hundred ringgit? Five? When the police come, you'll give them that statement, son," the old man says. His determined look leaves no room for questions or objections.

Mak Su, clearly not knowing what the conversation is about, caresses my face and nods. Warm tears fall on my forearm. "Do what your father says, Azraai," she says.

I exchange confused and worried glances with Vidya. Eventually, she, too, nods in agreement.

Well, the old man's right. The view from the room is great. I sit on the chair by the window and admire the clear night sky and the city lights. The twin towers of KLCC are alight, the pulsing heart of Kuala Lumpur, but the surrounding skyscrapers are not to be outdone. Even buildings under construction are well-lit. The lights of the hospital garden are turned on, including the ones along the path that leads to the helipad. If moving so much didn't cause me pain, I would have enjoyed catching some fresh air. Since the beginning of the movement control order, the air feels significantly less polluted. But it doesn't stop there. People are even showing photos of the river passing through Melaka city center where the waters are a clearer green, with fish gathering just under the surface instead of the usual teh tarik brown that we're used to. Maybe this is how nature repairs itself, by taking us out of the equation.

"You seem far away," Jacen says as he walks in. He's wearing a long-sleeved T and a pair of sweats.

"What are you doing here?"

He deposits his backpack on the sofa and walks over to sit on the chair across from me. "I told you I'd come back. Just needed to shower and pack fresh clothes and undies," he says matter-of-factly.

"Don't you have to work?"

"This is my first time claiming my leave allocation. Besides, I've got my shifts covered for the next three days, so I'm good. Why are you out of bed?"

"My butt ached from lying down too much. And the doctor has downgraded my pain meds to pills. Sucks, because the morphine was so good."

Jacen chuckles. "You're into drugs now?"

"If they make me feel that good, why not?"

"Man, KL is beautiful at night," he says as he stares out the window.

Framed by the soft light of the room and the illumination of the full moon, he's the beautiful one. His features are so defined, so unforgettable. Tearing my gaze away, I say, "Feels wasteful."

"What does?"

"Why keep *all* the lights on when most shops and businesses are still closed? Electricity isn't free."

"Maybe it's a symbol of hope that things will come back to normal soon."

"You're too positive for your own good," I say.

"And you're not?"

I give a one-sided shrug as an answer. After a few minutes of counting the lights in the garden, I finally ask, "Why did you stay over yesterday? And tonight?"

"That's what friends do."

"But we're not even close."

Jacen straightens my chair to face him directly. "Hey, listen. Do you know how terrified I was when I found out you were beaten up and unconscious? You know who did this."

It's not a question. I nod.

"Did it have to do with the video?"

Another nod.

"Tell me who they are. I'm going to beat those fuckers to a pulp."

"Let it go, Jace. It won't achieve anything. By the way, the things you said to my dad. Why did you do it? It was clearly me." I can't look at him when I say the last bit.

"To create reasonable doubt, enough to deny it's you. I want to major in journalism, remember?"

"He wasn't interested in listening to my side of the story," I say.

Jacen gently bumps his fists on my knees. "You don't see it, do you?"

"See what?"

"Your dad was protecting you. Aren't you the slightest bit curious why his assistant got a copy of the clip, too?"

Come to think of it, Jacen's right. But the thought of the old man protecting me is too much for my brain to handle. Some things are just impossible, and that's a fact.

"Azraai, there's one more thing," he says.

I look up at him. Jacen leans close, too close for comfort. My body stirs despite myself.

"About last Saturday night...."

"Forget it. I was drunk," I say.

"No, you weren't. *I* was."

"Exactly."

"Azraai, I was drunk, and you took me by surprise. I didn't want my actions to be that clouded," he says, his voice soft.

I look out the window. The full moon makes the entire sky brighter. The night's too beautiful to get my heart crushed again.

Jacen nudges my chin to face him. "Can we start over?"

"Start what over?"

He leans so close, our noses almost touch. "This. Can we try this again?"

"Jacen," I whisper. Why is my heart beating so hard? It's a good thing they've stopped monitoring my vitals.

"Call me what you called me just now."

I force my mind to be clear enough to think. What did I call him? "Jace?"

"Hmm..."

"You... you like girls."

He nods. Our nose tips brush together. "I like *you*," he says.

Jacen tilts his head, closes his eyes, and kisses me. He holds my upper lip between both of his and presses closer. He has the softest lips I've ever come across. He's also gentle, as if afraid of breaking me, as if unsure that I would reciprocate. His nose caresses mine as he parts my lips. The warm waves pulse from that single point and spread throughout my body, again and again, with each slightest movement.

I close my eyes and return the kiss.

13

I find myself smiling at the most random things at the most random time. Even when sudden movements bring renewed aches to my chest, the pain brings me back to that particular moment at the hospital. To the kiss.

Just remembering it makes me smile.

The doctor declared me fit enough to recuperate at home after three nights at the hospital. For the past two weeks at home, Mak Su has been mothering me with utmost vigilance. I'm not allowed to walk up and down the stairs unsupervised; even then she sets a limit of two trips at most a day. I'm not allowed to leave the house, but the good thing is that she brings all my meals to my room. That way, I don't have to face the old man.

He's made himself scarce after driving me home. He helped me up to my room, drew the curtains, looked at me as if he wanted to say something, but stopped himself and left. I've only seen hints of him ever since.

I keep thinking about what he did in the hospital ward. I don't think I've ever seen that side of him before, that commanding presence. The old man protecting me is not a theory that I buy.

Jacen. I smile again.

My phone beeps. I've set Jacen's personalized message and ring tones, so I immediately know it's him. We've been exchanging countless texts and late-night calls, talking about nothing and everything.

* * *

```
[Jacen] : Has Mak Su allowed you out of the house yet?
[Me] : Wasn't easy convincing her I'm fully mended.
[Jacen] : :D. Are you?
[Me] : Not all the way there yet, but don't tell her that.
Waddup?
[Jacen] : Want to catch a movie?
[Me] : Wingman duty? Again?
[Jacen] : …
[Jacen] : Just you and me.
[Me] : Like on an actual date?
[Jacen] : Maybe?
```

My healing cheek smarts when I grin, but I do it anyway.

```
[Me] : Do you need to bring a wingman?
[Jacen] : No? So are you game?
[Me] : I'm not allowed to drive.
[Jacen] : I'll park my bike at your place and we'll take
your car.
[Me] : Or I can take a Grab and meet you there.
[Jacen] : Share your location. I'm coming.
```

By the time I get ready, Jacen is already downstairs talking to Mak Su in Malay. From the bits that I can catch, he's trying to convince her that my comfort is his priority. To my surprise, he's wearing my batik shirt. He, in turn, raises an eyebrow when he sees me wearing his Starbucks collared T.

"Looks good on you, Azraai," he says.

"You actually cleaned it?" I ask.

"Took like three washes, but yeah. I cleaned it," he says.

Once Mak Su is convinced that no harm will come my way, Jacen helps me to the passenger seat, buckles my seatbelt, and before taking the wheel, he promises Mak Su one more time that he'll bring me straight home after the movie.

The mall is nearly deserted despite being close to the heart of KL. The stores that have reopened are all equipped with non-contact thermometers, either standing or handheld, their individual QR codes pasted at the storefront, and a bottle of hand sanitizer beside the door. Window shopping will be a chore from now on.

The cinema is in no better shape. Despite the reduced number of staff, there are more of them than moviegoers. After scanning the QR codes to check in using our phones, Jacen fiddles with his and shows his online purchase receipt to the usher.

Jacen leads me to the concession stand where a sleepy staff puts on her mask when we approach the counter. "Caramel popcorn and you're not sharing, right?" he asks.

Smiling, I nod. "That's right. Make it a large one. I've not had a snack since this happened," I say, waving at my face.

"Mineral water, diet soda, or is today your cheat day?"

"It's not like I can book a job anymore," I mumble. I have no idea how far they've circulated the video, and Dato' Hanis's words are a hammer in my head.

"What's that?" Jacen asks. He leans toward me and signals at my mask.

"Cheat day. Get me a proper soda," I say, louder.

We enter an empty hall, which is weird because the movie we're watching was just released last week, and the hype is still all over social media. When we take our seat in the middle, separated by a chair, Jacen leans toward me.

"Can I claim I booked the entire hall?"

Chuckling, I say, "Claim away. Not like you're scoring any points."

"I like this place because even before Covid, few people come here. Except during weekends," he says as he parks both popcorn boxes on the empty chair between us.

The lights turn off and advertisements roll in. I keep stealing glances at the closed doors to the sides behind us, expecting latecomers to surreptitiously enter, but by the time the movie starts, it's still just the two of us.

I reach for my popcorn at the same time Jacen takes his. Our hands brush and the fine hairs of my forearm stand in static. My jeans suddenly feel too tight, constricting.

My phone vibrates during the second act. When I see the sender, I raise my eyebrows and look to my right.

```
[Jacen] : May I try something?
[Me] : Why are you texting?
[Jacen] : May I?
[Me] : ?
```

Jacen reaches across the seat between us, takes my hand, and holds it where our popcorn boxes were. He intertwines his fingers with mine. He's so warm.

I end up eating using my left hand until the show ends. Jacen only releases me when the hall lights come back on.

I also end up smiling throughout an action movie.

True to his word, Jacen drives me home right after watching the movie. No pit stops, not even for a cup of coffee. It's pouring outside, and the sky is uniformly gray. Seeing that the rain doesn't show any signs of abating when Jacen parks the car on the porch, I invite him in. Jacen hesitates for a moment, but I'm sure he knows he's stuck here for a few hours at least. If I'm lucky, he'll even stay overnight.

As soon as I enter the front door, Mak Su swoops in and inspects me for any new bruises or aches. She keeps looking at Jacen, who's still hanging out at the doorway, as though waiting to be allowed in.

"Mak Su, we *watched* an action movie. We didn't make one. I'm fine, see?" I say.

"Jacen, stay for dinner, will you? Yusoff works late today, so it'll be just the three of us. You're a Buddhist? You don't eat beef, do you?" Mak Su asks.

"Thank you, but I don't want to impose. I'll be on my way once the rain stops," he says. His Malay is impeccable.

"No such thing. You're staying for dinner. End of discussion," Mak Su says.

Jacen looks at me, and I shrug. I find it easier to duck than to argue with Mak Su, but I'm not about to tell him that.

"Thank you, Mak Su. And no, I don't eat beef," he says. Smart guy.

Satisfied, Mak Su gives me a once-over before returning to the kitchen. She insists I give a tour of the house first, to make Jacen feel more at home, apparently, but I rather skip the pleasantries and go straight for something more pleasant instead. I lead him up the staircase, but he stops halfway to study the paintings on the wall.

"These landscape paintings are amazing. The paddy fields look so alive. And this beach view, it's just... wow. Local artists?"

I lean against the railing and nod. "My mom used to support local talents, and I guess the old man is continuing her efforts."

"You guys aren't close, are you?" he asks.

"How did you figure that one out, Jace?" I ask as dryly as possible.

"Well, you never call him your dad, but more than that, where are the family photos?"

"Oh. That."

"Sorry, I didn't mean to—"

I cut him off. "No, no. It's okay. Ever since the accident, I cannot recognize my mom's face. Show me any pictures, and hers is the only one I somehow can't *see*. Years of therapy still haven't cured that. So the old man decided it would be easier if he took down her photos. She was in every single one of them."

"Do you miss her?" Jacen asks, his voice gentle.

"I think I miss the idea of her. Mak Su feels like my actual mother. She's the one who raised me. The old man avoids me whenever he can."

"And it's not the other way 'round?"

I narrow my eyes and study Jacen. Few people notice that about me, mostly because I keep my private life private. "Are you planning to write an exposé on me?" I ask, half-joking.

"Maybe, once you reach a million followers," he says without missing a beat.

Jacen actually gawps when he enters my room. Not that it's worth gawping over. I lock the door behind me and watch him as he gives himself a tour of the room. He runs his fingers over the game titles on the shelf below the TV, and then moves on to the bookshelf beside my bed and reads the titles on the spines.

"Didn't peg you as a Fantasy person," he says. His head is tilted to the left as he moves from the top row downward.

"What did you think I read?"

He shrugs as he settles on one book and takes it out to read the back cover. "I don't know. Tom Clancy, Sidney Sheldon. Dan Brown, maybe? *Lord of Secrets*. Is this book good?"

"Best Fantasy I've read in a long time. Witty and sarcastic and just… gritty, I suppose. I'd lend it to you, but that's my only copy."

Jacen reads the first few pages before returning the book to the shelf. With his full attention still on the books, I stealthily approach him and push him to the bed. He lands on his side with an airy thump.

Laughing, Jacen repositions himself upright and props himself up using his elbows. "Azraai. What are you doing?"

I push Jacen back down and crouch on top of him. I comb his hair away from his forehead and bury my hand in his hair. "You're beautiful, you know that?" I say.

"That's the first time someone used the word to describe me, so… thanks?"

I lean closer until I can feel his warm breath on my face. He smells like caramel popcorn.

"Azraai, Mak Su is downstairs," he says. But he's not putting up a fight.

"I locked the door."

"I don't think—"

This time I cut him off with a kiss, tentative and teasing at first, then with more force. I cradle his head in both my hands as I part his lips with mine, making way for my tongue to slide against his. He whimpers when I playfully bite his lower lip. We trade kisses like almost competitive banter. Still on top of him, I release my hold on his head and move my hand downward. I trace a line on his neck, down his bobbing Adam's apple, to the groove at the base of his neck, and then roam his hard chest under the soft silk shirt. He gasps when I fiddle with his nipple. The fabric makes him even more sensitive.

"Azraai," he whispers between kisses.

I slip my hand under his shirt and trace the smooth muscular bumps of his abs, which he contracts, as though tickled. I travel lower and rest my hand on his hard-on under his tight jeans. I stroke its outline and he expands even more if that's even possible.

"Azraai, stop."

I deftly unbutton his jeans and push the zipper down. I slide my hand under the band of his underwear. My skin tingles from the heat he emanates.

Jacen grabs my hand and pushes me to the side. He gasps for air before zipping up his pants, which is a struggle for him because of his raging hard-on.

I lie on my side, looking at him. My breaths are just as ragged as his.

Jacen turns to his side to face me. "Can we take it slow? I don't know what I'm doing right now," he says.

"Go slow. Sure thing."

"You're not… mad, are you?"

I pull him closer and plant a quick kiss on his forehead. "I don't mind going slow. But I need to do something about this."

I take his hand and place it on my hard-on. His eyes widen, but it's more of a panicky look than an impressed one. I sigh, roll over, and rise from the bed.

"Where are you going?"

I point at my crotch. "Bathroom. I need to address this. Unless you want to help me out."

Jacen blinks at me. He doesn't know how to respond.

I huff a long sigh and lock myself in the bathroom. Turning on the sink to full blast, I drop my jeans and jack myself in front of the mirror. I climax in less than a minute, but I keep the tap on while I clean myself and the sink counter and the mirror, and wait for at least three more minutes before coming out. I don't want Jacen to think I can't last long.

Jacen is sitting at the edge of the bed, with the Epiphone on his lap. He looks at me; uncertainty is plainly written on his face. "You really…" he trails off and makes the jacking off gesture.

I lean against the doorframe. "Bathroom's all yours."

Blushing, Jacen shakes his head. He turns his attention to the guitar and gently runs his thumb over the strings. "This is the guitar you brought to the photo shoot?"

"My Epiphone? Yeah."

"You named your guitar?" he asks.

"Sort of. It's the name of the brand."

"So you're into labels?"

I feel like his question has a deeper meaning, but I brush the thought away. I sit beside him and take over the Epiphone when he hands it to me. "I don't really care about labels. This particular model is expensive for an acoustic guitar. I always wanted one for myself, but I waited until I earned enough money from modeling to buy this one. So I named it Epiphone to remind myself that I can make it on my own in case the old man kicks me out. Or if I cut myself off."

Jacen opens his mouth to say something but seems to change his mind. His lips are still red and slightly swollen from my rough administrations. "Play me a song," he says.

We're sitting so close our shoulders rub against one another. I like sitting like this. I like his warmth. While I think of a song to play, I strum the Epiphone. I decide to sing "Heather" by Conan Gray. I secure the capo on the fifth fret and strum the intro: C, Em, Am, Fmaj, Fm. Then I gently sing the song.

Jacen bumps my shoulder and clasps his fingers over mine on the fretboard. His fingertips are smooth, unlike my calloused ones. He turns his head to look at me. "Why do I have a feeling this is about my jacket?" he asks.

Smiling, I say, "Just switch Heather with Elayne."

"It's not even real leather. I'm sure you have real ones," he says, his face drifting closer.

"I know. But you liked her better."

"You want to know why she left early at that party? She kissed me, but I realized I wanted to kiss someone else. I forced myself to kiss her back, but it turned out all wrong. You're not half as pretty as she is, Azraai. You're a whole different league altogether." His voice is softer now, barely audible.

I surrender to the gravity that pulls us together. Our lips move in a gentle kiss, exchanging a wordless conversation. But eventually, we get hungrier, greedier. Jacen pulls away first.

"If we keep this up, I'll end up using the bathroom for real," he says.

"Well, we can help each other out. Or we can just jerk off together if you want to take it slow."

Jacen seems to be seriously contemplating that option, but the spell breaks when Mak Su gently knocks on my door. He scoots away in an instant, beyond my reach.

"Azraai, Jacen, come have dinner," Mak Su's muffled voice floats from outside.

"Coming," I call out.

The Epiphone still in my hands, I turn to face Jacen. He's adjusting his shirt to hide his hard-on as if afraid Mak Su will walk in on us.

He's just two scoots away, but right now, he feels a world apart.

The rain finally lifts after we finish dinner, and despite the wet, chilly night, Jacen insists on going home. He has to help his parents buy fresh produce at the market for their booth.

Jacen straddles his motorbike and fastens his helmet, but doesn't start the engine. He waits for me to say something, but when I don't, he says, "Once you're all better, maybe one of these weekends I'll bring you to my folks' booth. We sell pork, but I'll ask my dad to cook something suitable for you to eat."

"I'm not *that* strict about eating halal," I say, almost rolling my eyes.

"I know. That's why I'm offering."

"So you don't want to do anything more than kiss me, but you already want me to meet your parents. You're weird, Jace," I say.

Jacen winces and bites his lower lip. I don't know why, but seeing him absently play with his lips always sends a thrill down my spine.

"Give me some time to get used to this idea, okay? You're the first guy I've fallen for, and I'm not into any other guys, so let me wrap my head around this first. Please."

"What did you say?" I ask.

"Please?"

"No, before that."

"I'm not into guys?"

"Come on, Jace. You know what I'm talking about."

Jacen signals for me to come close, but instead of the kiss that I'm badly expecting, he playfully tugs at my nose. "I've fallen for you, Azraai Yusoff."

"Come on, no kiss?"

"Mak Su is just inside, Azraai. And the door is wide open."

"Seriously? Not even a peck on the cheek?"

Jacen gives me a brilliant grin, pumps the engine to life, and bumps his fist on my chest. Barely audible over the tinny sputter of the motorbike's engine, he says, "If I kiss you, I won't go home tonight."

Jacen rides away before I can talk him into staying the night. Maybe next time, then. I wait until his red rear light disappears before returning to the warmth of the house. Mak Su is sitting cross-legged on the carpet in the living room with her back against the sofa. She's watching her nightly Malay drama on TV while folding laundry fresh out of the dryer. Since the old man is not back yet, I decide to join Mak Su and lie down on the sofa behind her.

"Did you lock the door?" Mak Su asks, her attention on the TV. She doesn't have to look down to fold the clothes into perfect squares.

"Yes, Mak Su. I even latched it."

"Your father isn't back yet," Mak Su says, turning to face me. When she sees my grin, though, she gently slaps my forearm.

We watch the TV for a while. I ask Mak Su about the characters and what's happening, and she offers information as if trying to convince me to follow the series. I indulge her because I cherish these quiet moments, just the two of us.

"Jacen seems like a nice boy. Very courteous. And his Malay is surprisingly good," she says.

"I know, right? So good. He wants to take up journalism. Maybe he'll be a prime-time news anchor."

"He has the face for it. I like him."

"Mm-hmm," I hum.

"You like him too, don't you?"

"Mm-hmm."

"You *like* him, don't you?"

I understand Mak Su's emphasis, but I don't know how to respond. I freeze on the sofa, not even daring to breathe. Right now, I'm glad her eyes are glued to the TV. I don't want to see her disappointment.

"Does he like you back?" she asks, softly.

Wait. What is happening?

"I know what you've been hiding in your underwear drawer. You need to hide your stuff better. I won't lie. I'm worried about you, but I'm also thankful that you're being safe."

"You know?" I tentatively ask.

"You're like a son to me, Azraai. And a mother knows about these things. I was raised in a different time, a different environment, so I don't know how to talk to you about this. And I don't know if it's my place to say anything."

I bury my face in her shoulder. Before I can stop myself, I'm crying. I don't know why. I know exactly why.

Mak Su combs my hair with her fingers. "I hope he likes you more than you like him. Always love a person who loves you more."

"Did you have that with arwah?" I ask, referring to her late husband, who used to be the old man's driver.

"He loved me even though I couldn't give him any children. That says a lot about a man. You know a person loves you more when they are willing to sacrifice their future just to be with you, even when you don't want them to. Before he passed, he even gave me his permission to stay here for your sake, and he'd pay whatever the price in Afterlife," she says.

"Arwah's going straight to Heaven, Mak Su."

"Insya-Allah. I think so, too."

"I won't, though. I'm going straight down."

Mak Su turns and holds my face in her hands. "Why did you say that? Never say that, Azraai."

"Because of who I am, Mak Su."

"Allah creates each person exactly the way He means them to be, and He never makes mistakes. Don't let anyone have you believe otherwise. He just made your path a little harder, is all."

"So I'm not... *wrong*?"

Mak Su looks at me and pours all the love she has for me through her eyes. "You, son of my heart, are perfect."

14

It's a good thing I listened to Jacen when he told me to wear something comfortable. His family's booth is at a non-air conditioned hawker center in the middle of Cheras with big non-halal signage at the entrance. Red-and-white hazard tapes are used to cordon off the open spaces between the pillars all around the center, leaving a single area open as the entry and exit point. A QR code and a standing non-contact thermometer have been set up, and a RELA guard in full uniform mans the entrance. Despite the small fan whirring on his desk, sweat beads dot his entire face and neck.

Jacen meets me outside the entrance and leads me to an old motorbike instead of heading for his booth. He's carrying red plastic bags filled with styrofoam packages in both hands. Other than a warm hi, he doesn't offer me any form of physical contact. He hands me a helmet before putting on his own. He then carefully stacks the packages in a square metal container at the back of the bike.

"Where are we going?" I ask.

"I need to deliver these orders before the food gets cold."

"We can take my car."

"Weekend traffic is going to build up soon. The bike's faster," he says.

Grabbing his shoulders, I climb onto the bike and sit behind him. He takes my hand and places it on his waist.

"Hold on tight. Mak Su will kill me if you fall and hurt yourself," Jacen says as he twists the handle and revs the engine.

I rest my chin on Jacen's broad shoulder, but he twists away.

"Azraai, we're out in the open. People can see," he says.

Startled by his remark, I release my hold, but he grasps both my hands and puts them back on his waist.

"Sorry. I didn't mean to snap. People talk, and I don't want them to get the wrong idea," he says.

"And what kind of idea is that?" I ask, but he revs the engine harder. I don't think he can hear me over the din.

Jacen weaves through traffic with ease. Now I get why he prefers the motorbike even though it makes us look like delivery boys, which is, come to think of it, exactly what we are. I also get why he wanted me to wear something comfortable. Even though the wind whips at me as Jacen speeds along busy streets, the air on my exposed face, forearms, and lower legs feels super-heated. It's worse when we stop at traffic lights. Makes me realize how much I've taken the comfort of my car for granted.

"You do a lot of deliveries?" I ask after Jacen hands a middle-aged lady a plastic bag over closed gates at a single-story terrace house.

"We only started during the MCO when we had to close shop. We had to improvise after a month without income. My parents were initially against it, especially since they had to make do with our cramped kitchen at home, but my sisters offered to do the deliveries since they couldn't attend school, anyway. I help whenever I don't have classes or shifts at Starbucks," he says.

"Why not work with your family full time?"

Jacen laughs and restarts the engine. "This is their thing. Besides, I wouldn't be able to afford my tuition fees and school stuff for my siblings."

"What about public universities?"

Jacen turns to look at me sideways and grins. "Have you seen my skin? I'd have to take STPM and even then, the competition's stiff. And we wouldn't have met."

There's no rancor in his voice, but getting this small glimpse of Jacen's life makes me think about how privileged I have always been, and it's not a simple concept to swallow. Maybe I should visit Mama and talk this out with her.

We make three other stops before returning to the hawker center. Jacen is always courteous and calls his customers by name. Two of them, both teenage girls, ask about me, and Jacen simply says, "Pengyou." Friend. I just smile blankly when they look at me. I have to admit, it's fun watching them blush, just to catch that unease on

Jacen's face.

Jacen parks his motorbike farther away than his previous spot, and as I adjust my hair after returning the helmet, that uneasy look intensifies.

"What's wrong?" I ask.

"Azraai… I…"

"Come on, out with it. You've been a little off the entire day."

"The thing is…"

"You don't want anyone to know about us," I say without missing a beat.

Jacen's anguished look turns into guilt. His soft, very kissable lips are trembling. "I'm really, really sorry. My parents are old-fashioned."

"You're talking as if this *entire country* isn't old-fashioned," I say, dryly. "It's not like we're boyfriends, anyway."

Jacen stares at me as though I've just punched the air out of his lungs. "That's unfair."

Maybe what I said was unfair. But Jacen isn't the first straight guy who makes me feel like a dirty secret. Maybe coming here was a bad idea, after all. "I think it's better if I just go home," I say.

Jacen pulls the hem of my T-shirt as I turn to leave. "Don't. Stay. I *want* to introduce you to my family," he says.

"Why?"

"Because I'm hoping that they'll like you, and I'm hoping for you to like them back."

I turn to face him. "Why is that important to you?"

"Because you're important to me," he says.

I sigh and pocket my keys. How can I walk away from *that*?

I'm sure during pre-Covid times, this hawker center used to overflow with diners. Even TripAdvisor gives this place a 4.5-star rating. But right now, only a handful of booths are open, while the rest have their shutters rolled down and locked, with notices of varying sizes written in Chinese script pasted on the shutters. They chained foldable square tables and plastic chairs to pillars in front of each closed booth. Jacen tells me that some of them are permanently shut down or evicted, with no new tenants to take their place. I wonder how much worse the economy will be affected if this pandemic goes on.

Jacen leads me to a booth with overhead signage that reads QUAN ROAST PORK NASI LEMAK in both Latin and Chinese scripts. I raise an eyebrow at him. While nasi lemak is a staple among Malaysians, we eat the coconut rice with sambal, anchovies, a slice of egg, and peanuts, and the additional dish usually comprises chicken, beef, squid, or cockles.

Laughing, Jacen says, "We have chicken rendang too if you're wondering. And fried pork rice."

What I'm wondering is how well pork goes with nasi lemak, because the aroma alone is doing a number on my empty stomach. If one day I end up eating pork, this place will definitely be my first stop.

Even though Jacen's family's booth is one of the few that are operating, I can see only five dine-in customers, and one guy wearing a mask and playing with his phone sits near the food prep counter. A lanky boy with his mask below his nose sits at the farthest table, drawing on an A4-sized sketchbook. All the square plastic tables have red duct-taped Xs on two opposing sides. Behind the counter, a middle-aged man is busy tossing the rice in a huge wok, a lady is packing food into a styrofoam pack, and a teenage girl is arranging plates on a tray. I can see the family resemblance in their eyebrows and nose, but Jacen must have hit the gene pool jackpot extra hard.

Jacen introduces me to his parents in a dialect I can't catch. They smile and greet me as stiffly and awkwardly as I smile back at them. He leans close and whispers, "Sorry, my folks don't speak Malay that much, and no English at all."

"What kind of Chinese did you guys use just now?"

Jacen raises an eyebrow and gives me an amused look. "*What kind of Chinese?*"

I step on his shoe as surreptitiously as possible. "You know what I mean."

He laughs again. His voice carries throughout the sparsely populated hall. "Hokkien. My parents migrated from Penang when I was small. Wanted a better life for us here."

"You were born in Penang?" I ask.

Jacen takes out his wallet and shows me his identification card. "See there? 07. Penangite."

"You didn't tell me your birthday is coming soon. I'm older than you by three months. And that's you? Seriously?" I say, pointing at the black-and-white picture of the chubby boy with spiky hair.

He snaps the wallet closed. "Yeah, that was a mistake. Go make yourself comfortable. I'll bring you a plate of nasi lemak with chicken rendang."

"No pork?" I ask.

"Not on my watch, no."

"Do you need any help?"

Jacen's sister elbows him aside. "Hi, I'm Zhe Ling. My brother here didn't bother to introduce me. You are?" she says in rapid-fire English.

"Azraai. His friend from uni."

She looks up and studies me closer. "I think I've seen you on billboards and in magazines. You're famous, aren't you?"

I look at Jacen and give him a half-grin. "Your sister's got taste."

"Can I get a selfie with you? My friends are going to freak out when I tag you on Instagram," she says.

Smiling wider, I bend down to Zhe Ling's height as she takes out her phone and poses with a miniature heart sign. Placing my hand beside hers, I mimic her gesture and smile for the camera.

After a few shots, Jacen pulls her aside and says, "Azraai, don't encourage her. So, can you cook?"

I shake my head.

"Chop vegetables?"

"Nope."

I take the tray filled with two plates of nasi lemak and two plates of sliced roast pork from the counter before Zhe Ling can pick it up. "I can bring this food to the customer's table. Which one?"

Jacen shakes his head, but he's also smiling. He asks his mother in Hokkien, and then says to me, "See the aunties in the blue shirt and green T-shirt? That table."

Not wanting to embarrass myself, I carefully carry the tray and place it at a nearby empty table, and then gently place the food in front of the customers. The elderly ladies seem to be delighted that I'm serving them. They pat my forearm and call me a handsome boy in Mandarin. They also tell each other that I make them feel young again and then giggle, but I keep my amusement to myself.

The boy sitting alone beside a pillar catches my attention. I take the empty tray and head over to see what he's sketching, and I give a low whistle without thinking when I see him coloring a realistic rendering of Jupiter. I sit beside him and place the tray on an empty chair.

"Your Jupiter is amazing. You even have the moons. Are those Io and Europa? What about the other two?" I ask.

"Ganymede and Callisto. Did you know Jupiter has 79 moons?" he says in perfect Malay without looking up.

"Seriously? That many?"

"Saturn has 82, but I like Jupiter better," he says.

"What about Pluto? I love the picture that New Horizons sent back," I say.

He scrunches his face. "Pluto isn't a planet."

"Pluto doesn't get the love that it deserves. A dwarf planet, what's up with that?"

Jacen rushes to my side and tries to pull me away. "What are you doing?" he asks.

"Chatting about planets," I say.

Still coloring and not looking up, the boy says, "Pluto isn't a planet."

Jacen releases his grip and pulls a chair to sit beside me. He looks bewildered. "Zhe Jie doesn't talk to just anyone."

"He's your brother?" I ask. When I look closer, I realize how similar they look even though Zhe Jie doesn't have any of Jacen's bulk. I'm quite certain he'll eventually glow up as his brother did. I give my full attention to Zhe Jie. "Can I see your other artworks?"

He pushes the book toward me, and I slowly flip through the pages. His renderings of the planets in the solar system are brilliant, almost photorealistic, even. I comment on each of the planets and their moons, and Zhe Jie offers some trivia.

"You surprise me, Azraai. He doesn't even let *me* look at his drawings," Jacen says, his low voice filled with wonder.

"That's because you know nothing about the solar system," Zhe Jie says.

"You should frame these up. Maybe sell them. You've got serious talent, Zhe Jie. I like you," I say.

"Big Brother likes you," he says.

I look at Jacen, and his eyes widen in alarm. He whips around to see if anyone is listening in, but I ignore him and lean closer toward Zhe Jie.

"How do you know?" I ask.

"He video chats with you when he thinks I'm asleep, and he always smiles when he reads your messages."

I look sideways at Jacen and grin. He's full-on panicking, but he doesn't go over to physically stop his brother, even though he clearly wants to do just that. "Zhe Jie, what did we discuss about oversharing?" Jacen asks between gritted teeth.

"How did you know it was me?" I ask Zhe Jie.

"I recognize your voice. And he keeps looking at the picture of you. You're holding a guitar and he's holding a basketball. Do you play the guitar? Big Brother is an outstanding basketball player. But he doesn't know the names of the moons like you do," Zhe Jie says, almost absently.

Jacen pulls me away and forces me to sit at a table much closer to the counter. He kneels beside me and whispers, "Stay here and eat. And don't go over to my brother until I talk to him. *Please.*"

I give Jacen a smug smile. "You have a photo of us on your phone?" I whisper back.

Rolling his eyes, Jacen stands up and ruffles my hair. "Shut up, Azraai. And don't post photos of this place on Instagram."

"Why not? You've seen how my endorsement helps," I say.

"You want to promote a non-halal place and have your fans turn on you? Come on, you know how this works. This is Malaysia."

Well, he got me there. Once he hands me my lunch, Jacen continues to help his parents. I don't understand what they're saying, but their warm exchanges and laughter tell me how close they are. Halfway through my meal, one aunty approaches the counter to pay for her food. She speaks in Mandarin, and Jacen's mother replies in kind. I don't mean to eavesdrop, but they're talking so comfortably and loudly, it's impossible to *not* hear their conversation.

"Is this your eldest?" the aunty says.

"Yes, yes. He's in university. The first one in the family," Jacen's mom says.

"He's so tall and handsome. How many girlfriends do you have, boy?"

Without moving my head, I steal a glance at Jacen while I eat. He blushes and nods, but says nothing.

"What are you waiting for? Find a good girl, get married, and have beautiful children. How many do you want to have?" asks the aunty.

"He's going to give me four grandchildren and make me a proud and happy grandmother. What about the girl who came to the house yesterday? The pretty one with the copper hair," his mother says.

Jacen immediately looks at me, but I continue chewing as if I don't understand a single word. He gives a sigh of relief and flashes a weak smile at me.

I smile back but wonder if Zhe Jie can draw the supernova taking place in my head. No. Make it a black hole of conflicting feelings.

Jacen invites me for a stroll around the area after I finish eating. I walk a step behind him, lost in my thoughts. I want to ask him about Elayne, but I don't know how to form the words. I've never really asked him if he broke up with her, and as I said earlier, we're not even boyfriends. The only thing I know is that he likes me.

"Zhe Jie speaks good Malay," I finally say. The memory of the conversation with Jacen's brother is the only thing that's keeping me tethered right now.

"And you pronounce his name like a native Mandarin speaker. People say our names are difficult to pronounce because they don't sound like how they're spelled," he says.

I shrug off the compliment. "He doesn't go to a Chinese school like you did?"

"The social worker assigned him to a special needs school because he cannot socialize with others. His lessons are mostly in Malay, so one day he conversed exclusively in Malay. Imagine my folks' frustration when they couldn't communicate with him."

Curiosity banishes the dark questions from my head. "Is that why your Malay is flawless, too?"

Jacen chuckles. He stops, takes out his phone, and snaps a picture of grilles on a closed shop front. "You noticed that?" he asks.

"Even Mak Su was impressed."

"I forced myself to learn the language well for Zhe Jie. Plus, it'll give me an edge when I look for work. English, Mandarin, *and* Malay."

"Always thinking about the future," I absently say.

Jacen turns to face me and starts walking backward. "The future is everything to me. It's all I have. I want a better life for my family. By the way, what you did with my brother back there, that was… unexpected."

"What, when he told me you liked me?"

"No, that was… I need to talk to him about that," he says.

"Or stop assuming he doesn't pay attention when you talk to me on the phone," I say, smiling.

"That, too. But he doesn't talk to strangers. Or even other relatives."

"It's just my luck we have a common interest, I think."

"Not just that. He likes you," he says.

"But not the way you like me."

Jacen reaches over and ruffles my hair again. "Will you let it rest? Hey—"

My phone rings. It's my agent. I pick it up immediately.

"Are you available on Tuesday? I already told them you and Vidya will do it, so free your schedule," my agent says. No greetings, no exchanging pleasantries, just calling to tell me he's accepted a gig without checking with me first. In a way, I'm glad that hasn't changed.

"What kind of job?" I ask.

"Dato' Hanis has a new batik line. It's a photoshoot. I'll text you the time and location."

When he disconnects the call, I stare at the screen and blink instead of breathe. "I can't believe it. My modeling career is not dead," I say.

"Why should it be?" Jacen asks.

I tell him about Zakry, and how he committed career suicide when he recorded the sex video in the first place, knowing its existence alone could threaten his future. When my clip was distributed, I feared I would face the same fate. Jacen doesn't ask for details, but the look on his face fills me with unease.

"You wanted to say something just now?" I ask to break the weighty silence.

"Nothing. It's stupid."

"What? Tell me."

Jacen scratches his temple and looks away. "We've never taken a picture together," he says.

"Jealous of your sister? Or are the photoshoot pictures not enough for you to stare at anymore?"

"Are you going to be this impossible all day?"

I laugh and take out my phone. I hold it slightly upward after setting the front-facing camera. "Come on. The lighting's nice. Not too harsh."

Jacen stands beside me awkwardly. His smile looks forced. The candid shots of him I've been secretly taking are amazing and natural. He seriously needs to learn to be comfortable in front of the camera if he wants to be a journalist. I sling my arm over his shoulder and pull him closer. Jacen immediately looks around.

"Relax. We're two friends taking a photo together. There's nothing weird about that," I say.

Jacen visibly relaxes, and when he does, his face really is beautiful.

15

"Come on, Vid. What's taking you so long? We're going to be late," I say, staring at my wristwatch for the tenth time in two minutes. I plop on Vidya's bed and check my I-G feed. More and more people are doing throwback holiday posts. It's kind of sad.

"Never rush a woman," Vidya calls out from within her walk-in closet.

"That's why I came two hours early. But you're still gonna make us late. You're not doing your makeup, are you? They're gonna do it on-set."

Vidya steps out, holding a top in each hand. I point at the neon-yellow one with a plunging neckline.

"Why rush? Aren't you her new Zakry? I'm sure they'll hold off everything until you make your entrance," she says before walking back in.

I look at my watch again. It won't slow down no matter how much I will it to. Sighing, I rise from her bed, straighten it, and peek into the closet. "I'm getting something to drink. If you're not downstairs in fifteen minutes, I'm leaving without you," I say.

Vidya waves me away. I walk down to the kitchen to get chilled water from the dispenser and politely decline one of the maid's offer for some munchies. I did not do all these pull-ups last night to be defeated by snacks, even the expensive, directly-flown-from-Abu-Dhabi kind.

While I finish my drink and do my best not to stomp back up to forcibly drag Vidya to the studio, Rohan walks into the kitchen in a navy-blue pinstripe suit and a shimmering white-on-blue polka-dot tie. His curly hair is slicked back, and his beard is neatly trimmed. He looks absolutely scorching.

"You can close your mouth now, Azraai," Rohan says, chuckling as he tries to fasten his cufflink. "Help me with these?"

I take the chrome cufflinks from his hand and slot them in. Not only does he look good, but he also smells even better. He has a foresty scent with a hint of spice. I'm not surprised if his perfume is tailor-made for him, just like his suit.

"What are you guys up to?" he asks.

"A photoshoot gig for Dato' Hanis," I say.

"Her designs are pretty good. Some of my friends talk about getting her to design their wedding gowns. As I recall, you looked great in that wedding ensemble. What's it called? Baju Melayu?"

"The only times I'll ever wear wedding outfits are for photo shoots and fashion shows," I say.

"If you don't have anyone in mind in, say, five years, you and I can get married in the US. Granted, I prefer an open marriage, but it'll be fun. I promise."

Thing is, I can't tell if Rohan is teasing me or if he's being serious. "Thanks for the offer. But I'm good. For now."

Rohan raises an eyebrow as he takes a sip from a freshly brewed cup of black coffee. "Not running away anymore?"

"No French words today?" I ask back.

"Are you telling me my French worked on you? Do you *want* me to speak French?"

"No, and I appreciate it if you don't," I say before ducking away to wash my glass, much to the discomfort of the maid.

Vidya finally walks in. She's wearing a yellow blouse and a pair of high-waisted black billowing pants. At least she made all that waiting worth it. "Rohan, are you hitting on Azraai again?"

"Should I stop?" he asks, grinning. He should stop doing that. It's almost as arresting as his French.

"Go disturb someone else. Aren't you late for work?" Vidya says. She takes a long sip from Rohan's cup.

"Not as late as you'll be," he says.

"I trust Azraai's driving skill. Right, babe?"

I rush to the front door after giving Rohan a quick wave. I won't be able to make it to the photo shoot if I ogle at him any longer.

We end up waiting almost half an hour for Dato' Hanis to come.

When she does make an entrance, all eight talents stand in a row with our masks off for her to inspect and choose as her principal models. She approaches the girls first and turns Vidya around before choosing her as the lead female model. Vidya gives me a mixture of an excited and smug grin. I guess her subtly elegant no-makeup-makeup look impresses Dato' Hanis.

When she goes over to the guys, she stops in front of me and nudges my face left and right to inspect it. "Good, no permanent scar. I heard you injured your face," Dato' Hanis says. She then backtracks and chooses another talent to be her lead guy. He's a first-timer, and nowhere near as good-looking as I am. I pretend not to see the shock on Vidya's face.

We proceed with makeup and fitting. The overall atmosphere is more subdued, and the makeup artists don't chat as much as the last time. Apparently, two crew members contracted Covid, and the burly Sis who did my makeup is on ventilator support. They got it from a high-profile event a month ago. Hearing about people getting infected is one thing. Finding out that someone I know is struggling for their life because of the virus hits too close to home.

Vidya is brilliant, and the dresses suit her skin tone perfectly. The new guy, however, is a total mess. He needs more directions than Jacen did, up to a point where Dato' Hanis stops the photoshoot midway and promotes another model to take the lead. The cameraman suggests my name, something no one has ever done before, judging from the uniformed surprise on all the staff members' faces, but Dato' Hanis ignores him completely.

Once the session ends and we've changed out of our outfits, I approach Dato' Hanis to thank her for hiring me. She leads me to the office, and the studio staff clears the room for us.

"What did I tell you? Never pull a Zakry on me, but you did it anyway." Dato' Hanis says once the door shuts behind the staff.

I didn't know that the clip has reached her knowledge. She didn't choose me as the lead, so I suspected as much. "I'm sorry. Someone took a—"

"I didn't want to hire you, you know. I don't like having rumors surround my campaigns. The most important thing for me is keeping my brand clean."

"Then why did you?" I ask.

She sits behind the desk and leans back. She stares at me, her long-lashed eyelids barely blinking. "So beautiful. Such a waste. You could have gone far with my brand. Zakry came just now to beg for another chance, you know. It's a sad thing to see beautiful people beg. They lose their beauty, their power, their advantage."

I don't know where this is leading, but I don't like it. Mental note: if Dato' Hanis offers me another gig, I need to give my agent a standing order to decline.

"Unlike you, Zakry doesn't have an influential parent to intervene on his behalf."

Wait. What does the old man have anything to do with this?

"Your father brought you to my attention in the first place, you know. And he assured me it wasn't you in the video, so I had nothing to worry about. I didn't grow up with your privilege. I earned my place the hard way, and it's difficult to be a woman in a man's world. Actions have consequences, and you need to learn that lesson. I will keep hiring you, but if other labels want you, I won't stop them. But if you stay, you'll need to earn my trust again. And I don't trust easily after someone breaks it. Understood? Oh. And. I saw you taking photos with Vidya during the shoot. Don't use any of them in your social media accounts."

I've never wanted to run away from anything as much as I do right now. Dato' Hanis thinks she can bring me to my knees? Fuck this shit. Fuck modeling.

"One more thing. If you make a scene or talk bad about my label in any way, I'll make sure no one hires Vidya, too. Her parents are nowhere near as powerful as your father, you know," she says as she inspects her manicured nails.

So this is why she hired Vidya. Fuck Dato' Hanis. I ball my fists until my nails bite into my palm. The pain is good. It keeps me centered. "I won't disappoint you again, Dato'," I say.

While we walk to my car, I listen to Vidya as she praises the outfits she had on during the photo shoot. This is the first time she worked for Dato' Hanis's label, and she can't stop talking about it.

"Babe, everyone said you should have been the lead guy," she says, but just like the entire conversation, I barely register whatever she's been telling me. "Babe? You okay?"

I smile and nod. "Just tired. And the makeup artist who did my face during our previous shoot is in the hospital for Covid."

"Oh. Babe. How's he doing?"

"Not good, I heard," I say, my voice low.

That ends our conversation. We walk in silence, both lost in our thoughts. I parked my car a short distance from the three-story building, and as we approach the parking lot, I spot Zakry leaning against the wall, vaping. White smoke billows from his mouth and nostrils. He seems different. Leaner, hardier. His hair is longer, too. He has it tied in a messy man-bun. He's still as good-looking as I remember, but it's as if he's lost his youth. Zakry looks like a grown-up who's had one too many beatings. I veer off toward him, and when Vidya notices his presence, she follows suit.

"Hey, Zakry. It's been... forever," I say.

"Still with Vidya, I see," Zakry says with a half-smile. "You guys look good. Did you have a photoshoot or something?"

"Yes. Dato' Hanis's batik line. That woman is amazing," Vidya says. She takes out her phone to show Zakry the pictures she took during the shoot.

"What are you doing here?" I ask.

"Had something to do nearby. Booked a Grab, but the driver just canceled. Guess I need to book another ride," he says after taking a long drag. The wind blows the smoke my way. It smells like rose syrup.

"Want me to give you a ride? I'll send Vid home first, then we can hang out or something," I say.

"Yes, come with us. Azraai is a five-star driver. He listens when you chat, and he knows his way around town," Vidya says. She subtly takes a step back to move away from the vape smoke.

"I don't want to intrude," Zakry says.

"You're not intruding, promise," I say.

Zakry pockets his vape, dusts the seat of his jeans, and follows us to my car. He sits at the back, and I keep stealing glances at him as I drive to Vidya's house. Sometimes he stares back, but most of the time he looks out the window. When I drop her off at her front steps, Zakry takes over the passenger seat. He says nothing until after we leave the gated community compound.

"It must be nice, being that rich," he says absently. "Hey, can I smoke in here?"

I lower both front windows. "Vape away."

"Thanks," he says. He offers me a drag, but I decline.

"So, where were you headed?" I ask.

"I was supposed to meet my boyfriend, but... I don't know. I don't feel like it," he says.

"Want to grab something to drink? I know a nice, quiet cafe near to here."

"Sure thing," he says. He takes another long drag and then exhales sideways out the window.

"Dato' Hanis told me you came to see her," I say.

"That bitch doesn't know when to keep her ugly mouth shut," he says. He looks straight ahead. It's hard to read his face.

"How's life after…"

"The sex tape? You're lucky yours didn't show your face. Did the guy force you to swallow? That was fucked up, man."

"You know about that?" I ask.

"Yeah. Saw it once, but the video somehow disappeared from the internet. I bet you can still find mine if you Google it," he says.

"Couldn't you just deny it or something? People do it all the time."

"Who would want to listen to someone like me? I'm nobody. I didn't even finish college. And did you know that my family kicked me out after finding out what I did? What I am?"

"Fuck, man. I'm sorry. I didn't know things got so… bad."

Zakry sits up and takes my phone. He keys in a destination in my navigation app. "Forget that drink. I want to show you something," he says.

"Show me what?"

"My life."

After driving for forty minutes, the app leads me to a row of shop lots near the outskirts of Subang. Other than a supermarket near the main road, the place looks deserted. Zakry instructs me to drive up the incline and park under the shade of a gigantic tree near the end of the row. I say nothing as he leads me to a unit fronted by old and faded wooden double doors. The stained glass panels are speckled with grime and dust.

"What is this place?" I ask. The unit to the left looks like a closed office, and the unit to the right has several red bills pasted haphazardly on its shuttered front. A stray dog sleeps on the cement floor nearby. The breeze brings a faint whiff of garbage and petrol. I can't help but feel as though I'm in a horror movie where I'll get chopped to bite-sized pieces once I'm inside.

"You'll see," Zakry says with a smile that doesn't quite reach his eyes.

Surprisingly, the door opens with barely a sound. Zakry steps into the dimly lit building, and I follow closely behind him. A plump middle-aged Chinese man sits behind a narrow counter. He stands up and welcomes us in English with an accent that I'm not familiar with. No, he's not Chinese. Vietnamese, maybe?

A white panel wall covers the entire space behind the counter, with a wooden office door at the far end, making the area look even more cramped. There's not even space to place any chairs or tables. There are no labels or signages on the panel. Everything looks so unassuming, it makes me even more suspicious.

"Welcome, welcome. Zakry, you brought a friend. He's delicious," the man says. Nope, not creepy at all.

"Is he here?" Zakry asks.

"Yes. He arrived like ten minutes ago?" he says.

I lean close and whisper at Zakry. "Seriously. What is this place? Where's the QR code and temperature checkpoint?"

The man behind the counter scoffs as if I were a particularly slow child. "Your cover fee is already paid for. Your friend here… this your first time to this kind of place? I'll let you in for free, but don't tell the boss," the man says. He hands us each a key. The number 14 is written on mine. He then presses a button and the door at the end unlocks. "Enjoy your stay, boys."

Zakry leads me past the door, down a narrow and dark corridor, and into a locker room that smells like damp towels and musk. He opens his square locker and takes off his clothes. "Come on, take everything off," he says.

I raise my eyebrows. "Everything?"

Zakry smirks at me as he hooks his thumbs over the band of his black shorties. He pulls down his underwear without reservation. "Everything. You can keep your mask on, but everything else goes."

I'm not ashamed of my body, but we don't strip naked in public here in Malaysia. Not even in gym locker rooms, where the shower stalls are individually covered with at least a curtain. Self-conscious, I slowly peel off my clothes, fold them, and stack them over my shoes in the small locker.

"You've buffed up a little. And nice trim. Were you expecting any action at the photo shoot like we used to do?" Zakry says. He has lost some of his bulk. His muscles are well-defined, but he's not as glorious to stare at as he had been back when he was modeling. He also has some old bruises on his back and sides.

"Are you going to tell me why we're standing here naked?"

Zakry gives a low laugh. "Come on, live a little. You'll like it. You'll see. It's dark out there, so just follow me. We're still early, so I don't expect a crowd."

He leads me through a different doorway, and the new corridor is even darker, illuminated by a red light that's almost black. It feels like we're walking in a maze with occasional nooks that have showerheads jutting out from the tiled wall. We walk up a staircase, and I can see a gym at the far end of the floor. It's the only well-lit space I've seen here so far, and clear floor-to-ceiling glass panels separate the gym from the rest of the facility. Someone is inside lifting a barbell, and he's *naked*. Like, who wants to show off his shriveled balls to the world while he lifts weight? And isn't he worried about snagging his dick while working out? I shudder at that thought.

Zakry takes a peek inside each windowed door on both sides of the corridor. I glance at one panel and see a couple of older men having sex. It finally dawns on me what this place is. What did I get myself into? Fuck.

Not finding what he's looking for, Zakry leads me up another staircase. They have divided this floor into two compartments. The steam room has a big CLOSED notice on the door. The other one is a sauna, which, I think, is just as bad as the steam room in transmitting Covid. I don't even want to think about the transmission of *other* diseases in this place.

Once inside, I realize why the sauna's not closed. The heat is minimal. A big-sized man sits at one end, his chest hair matted with sweat. He looks to be in his forties, maybe early fifties, from the white strands on his head and chest. And bush. He acknowledges our entrance with a nod. Two other men are inside, fondling each other. They look like they could use the gym facilities downstairs. Sweat rivulets trickle down their flabby paunch. They immediately perk up when they see us and adjust their position to display their sad hard-ons.

Standing in the middle of the room, Zakry turns to face me and whispers, "Take off your mask."

"Why?"

"Or not. Doesn't matter." He leans close and starts grinding against me. As we sweat, his movements become slicker, smoother, and he slowly gyrates on my body. He grabs my butt and pulls me even closer. He kisses my neck.

The two men jack off to the show we're giving them. The big man looks at us through slit-like eyes. He seems to be asleep or disinterested, but his hand slowly roams his body and thighs.

"What is this shit?" I ask Zakry for his ears alone.

Zakry kisses my jaw and playfully bites my earlobe. "See that big man? He's my boyfriend. My sugar daddy, actually. He likes to watch. I give him a show, I go down on him, I make him happy, and he gives me a place to stay, a really cool SoHo unit that he promised to transfer under my name. And he gives me money to buy things. Food, clothes, watches."

"What about your safety? I saw those bruises."

"Nothing is free," he says. Zakry shrugs and then twists to grind against me from the back. He positions his hard-on to slide between my ass cheeks. Despite myself, I'm getting hard. He reaches over from behind me and strokes my dick. Fuck, my head's getting cloudy.

The two men crawl on their knees toward us and start sliding their hands along our sweaty legs. I try to shrug them off, but Zakry grinds faster and pumps his dick between my thighs. He uses one hand to stroke me, and the other hand moves up to play with my nipples. Oh, fuck. The big man spreads his leg and starts stroking himself. With surprising agility, he rises from the corner and slithers toward us. He's about Zakry's height, but his bulk is overpowering. So is his musk. He pulls Zakry's hair and forces him to his knees. Zakry takes his dick in his mouth. The man pushes until Zakry gags, but he keeps pushing deeper.

Emboldened, the two men grope my body. One of them takes my dick in his mouth. I gasp sharply. Fuck, this is not right. I push the men away. They look surprised, but within seconds, they're both smiling. They must think I'm playing a game with them. I turn to look at Zakry. His face is still partially buried in the big man's bush. I take a step toward him, but he holds his hand up to stop me. His eyes are pleading.

The only way I can help Zakry is to escape this hell on my own without causing a commotion.

16

After texting to make sure Zakry was safe later that night, I locked myself in my room for three days. I took a shower every time I thought about what happened at the sauna, but no amount of scrubbing could remove the memory of the older men's filthy hands and mouths roaming my body. I don't know how many times I just lay on the shower floor with the water running until my shaking hands shriveled. I felt as filthy as those men, and I ended up showering again. And again.

Keeping myself hostage didn't help. Not answering any of Jacen's and Vidya's and Mak Su's texts and calls didn't help. Not coming out of the room when Jacen came on the second day didn't help. What I did and didn't do in those three days made matters worse. Everyone was worried about me. But I couldn't face any of them.

"So that's why I'm here, Ma. I need to talk to someone. I know this is not something you should talk about on hallowed grounds, but you'll put in a good word for me, won't you?" I ask.

A gigantic cluster of clouds block the sun, and for a while, I sit beside Mama's grave in its shadow. It's going to rain soon. I absently clear away fallen leaves and rub off mud smears from the granite curb surround while I think.

"Why did Zakry have to choose that path? There have to be other ways to make money. If he had come to me, I would have offered the empty guest room. I don't get it, Ma."

As usual, I don't get the answers I'm searching for. But at least talking to Mama helps. The memory still makes me involuntarily shiver, but I don't feel so dirty anymore. I recite al-Fatihah under my breath before leaving her grave.

Lost in thought, I almost bump into the old man on my way to the car. I sidestep, but he holds my forearm to stop me.

"Suzita told me you were not eating the last few days. You didn't even leave your room. Is everything all right, son?"

I want to ask him about what Dato' Hanis told me, but I'm already spent. I don't have the energy left for a confrontation. "I'm okay," I say.

"I'm glad you still visit your mother. Want to go back there with me so we can recite Yaasin for her together?"

I shudder as I shake my head. "No, thanks. She's all yours."

I take a step forward, but the old man tightens his grip. He's careful not to cause me pain, but I can't move without hurting us both.

"Son, you know you can talk to me about anything, right?"

"Let go," I say.

As soon as the old man releases his hold on me, I storm off toward my car and drive away without looking back. I head for Starbucks, knowing that Jacen is working. I haven't seen him since the day I met his family. Video calls don't count. Maybe talking to him will help clear my head. He tends to do that. He keeps me grounded, somehow.

I circle the building twice before finding an available parking spot. Within two minutes after I text him, he knocks on the window of the passenger seat. I unlock the door to let him in.

Jacen climbs in and closes the door. He keeps his eyes on me as though I'd disappear if he turned away. "It's good to see you, Azraai. You got us all worried. Are you all right?"

I lean back and turn my head to face him. He takes my hand and grips it tightly. "I am now. I miss you."

"I'm here, Azraai. I'm always here. Talk to me. I only have ten minutes, so why don't you come inside? I'll brew your usual drink, and I can drop by to check in on you," he says.

I close my eyes and try to breathe in Jacen's scent. "Soon. I just want to stay like this. Is it too much if I ask you to hold me and hug me here?"

"We're out in the open."

I give a long sigh. "Exactly. Never mind, forget it. Just don't let go of my hand. Not yet."

"Hey, are you okay?"

I nod, and after a minute of listening to the low rumble of the engine and the drone of air-conditioning, I tell Jacen about Zakry. He listens without interrupting or making any sounds. I ask him the same thing I asked Mama.

"Maybe he doesn't have a choice," Jacen says after another quiet minute. "Maybe taking that path means surviving."

"There must be other options," I say.

Jacen doesn't answer. He rubs my fingers with his, and circles the calluses on my fingertips as if fascinated by them. He takes out his phone and snaps our intertwined hands. "Hey. Let's head in. I'll make you a cup of hot chocolate," he says.

I scrunch my nose. "I don't like sweet stuff."

"You need the energy. You can't run on caffeine alone. I'll get you a bowl of mushroom soup as well. You know, comfort food."

"You can be my comfort food," I say. I smile at him.

Jacen smiles back. "You're impossible, you know that?"

I follow him in and sit at a quiet corner away from the lunchtime crowd. He comes over after a few minutes to place a cup of hot chocolate and a bowl of creamy mushroom soup on my table.

"Take your time, get some food in your stomach. I'll be back in a bit. Do you need any Sudoku? Or my jacket?"

I roll my eyes at him. "You're the one who's impossible."

I don't know how long I sit there, playing with my food, not really eating, when Vidya drags a chair to sit across from me. I blink at her. I take several moments to register her presence.

"Vid, what are you doing here?"

Vidya leans back and crosses her arms. "Jesus fucking Christ, babe. You couldn't answer my texts or pick up my calls? What did Zakry do to you?"

"How did you know I'm here?"

"Your boy Quan. He's worried about you."

I turn to look at him preparing a drink behind the counter. He looks so good, even from this distance. "He called you? You guys talk about me?"

"Maybe we should start a club. Oh, wait. You already have a fan club. Are you going to tell me what happened? Go get me a matcha latte before you do that. Getting ready in under ten minutes was hard work," she says.

"So it *is* possible for you to get ready in under two hours?" I ask, smiling. I rise from my chair and head to the counter to order Vidya's drink. Jacen is manning the cashier counter, and I say to him, "Thanks for calling Vidya."

Jacen shrugs. "I can't stay there with you because the drive-through and delivery orders are coming in like crazy. Besides, she's worried about you, too. She's a good friend," he says.

When I return with the drink, Vidya leans farther back and shifts her gaze from me to Jacen and back to me. "Is there something going on between the two of you I'm not aware of?" she asks.

"What makes you say that?"

"I don't know. The way you looked at each other, it's like nothing else existed. Plus, he was even more worried about you than I was, and that's saying a lot."

I sit down and take a sip from my cup. I stare at Jacen. When he glances our way, he flashes a brilliant smile.

Vidya leans forward and narrows her eyes. "Something *is* going on, isn't there? How come you didn't tell me? I'm offended, babe. Seriously."

I give a one-sided shrug. "I don't know. He won't use the term boyfriend even though I've mentioned it twice. And there's the Elayne situation."

"What situation?"

I tell her about the conversation I overheard, and I also tell her I don't think it meant anything, but Vidya doesn't agree.

"So he doesn't want to commit to a relationship with you, and most probably he hasn't broken up with Elise," she said.

"Elayne."

"Whatever. He's making you his side boo, and you're okay with it?"

I shake my head. "It's not that simple, Vid. You know how it works."

"Well, it should be simple. Just you wait. For Christ's sake, Azraai. You deserve better than this." Vidya fiddles with her phone and after a few minutes of intense concentration, her brows unknot and she gives a triumphant grin. "There. All set."

I open my mouth to ask her what she means by that, but my phone dings. It's a notification from I-G saying that Vidya tagged me in a post. I open the app to see the photo of Jacen and me looking at each other during the shot that feels like a lifetime ago. Both of us are tagged in the photo. "When did he and you become I-G friends?" I ask.

"When you were high on morphine. Now his post makes sense. People should *always* caption their posts," she says.

The photo is innocent enough, but my eyes widen in horror when I read the caption:

* * *

Vidya_Chastain Love is love. #BL #visibility #lovewins

"Vid, what did you do? Take it down," I say, but when I refresh the feed, it has already raked over two thousand likes, and comments filled with heart emojis.

I whip around when I hear a commotion at the counter. Jacen initially wears a confused look on his face, but when he checks his phone, the look turns much darker than the clouds over Mama's grave. He storms toward us and looms over Vidya.

"What the hell, Vidya? Do you have any idea what you *fucking* did?" he asks. He's trembling.

"You'll thank me later, Quan," she says, her tone both dismissive and defensive.

"Take it down, Vid. Please," I say. If I don't do something, their confrontation is bound to escalate into something ugly.

"Take it. Fucking. Down, Vidya. Now," Jacen says between gritted teeth. His fists are balled, and the muscles in his arms are tense.

I jump up and stand between them. I hold Jacen's shoulders and tighten my grip, hoping to shake him off his angry haze. "Jace, chill. She didn't mean any harm."

Jacen twists and slaps my hands away. "Tell your girl to take it down, Azraai, or else…"

It's suddenly my turn to get angry. *No one* threatens people I care about and gets away with it. Not even Jacen. "*You* calm the fuck down, Jace. You're making a scene," I say, my voice controlled.

Which is true. The entire cafe is looking at us. Everyone's deathly quiet. The only sounds I can hear are the hum of the building and the pings of incoming delivery orders. At least the staff has some sense to continue working when I look their way.

"Too late. The damage is done," Jacen says. He shows me his phone. He's getting a huge amount of follow requests and DMs.

"What's so wrong with that?" I ask.

"You don't get it, do you? You asked me why your friend did what he did because there's no way in hell that you could comprehend his situation. Do you have any idea how fucking sheltered, how privileged you are?"

His words feel like a punch to my gut. I back away half a step. Vidya holds my hand.

But Jacen is not done. "Have you checked if your video is still online? Has the university taken action against you? You were worried you'd be out of a job, but you still got the gig. Even if you don't get to model ever again, your future is already set."

I hate that Jacen's right. But I hate that he's throwing this in my face even more. "So what, Jacen?"

He scoffs and raises his arms halfway before dropping them. He slumps on my chair and covers his face with his still trembling hands. *"So what?* You get no more privileged than that. Haven't you realized people like your friend, people like me, don't have that same luxury? Vidya's post is as good as kissing my future goodbye. I'm screwed, Azraai."

"Is that why you haven't broken up with Elayne?" I ask.

Jacen looks up at me. Confusion is written all over his face. "What are you talking about?"

I switch to Mandarin. "You didn't tell me she came to your house. And your mother is hoping to have four grandchildren from you guys."

"You know how to speak..." he trails off.

"You're not the only one who's fluent in English, Malay, *and* Mandarin, Jacen. I've been learning the language since kindergarten."

"That's unfair, Azraai. How come you didn't tell me?"

I throw my hands up. "Does it even matter? You were courting me, but you kept her as your backup plan," I say. When Jacen whips around to see if anyone's listening in, I squat down in front of him. "This. This is exactly what I mean. I don't want to be your dirty little secret, Jacen. There's nothing wrong or abhorrent about loving another man. I want to love in the light, not hide in the darkness. And you're afraid of your own shadow."

"Hypocrite. Have you actually told the world that you're *gay*? I saw your face when your father watched the clip. He doesn't know, does he? And what about Vidya? There's not a single post about her love life, but she's allowed to *expose* me?"

Jacen throws the words at me as though they were a condemnation. I close my eyes, inhale, and then exhale slowly. I switch back to English. "You're right, Jacen. Vidya had no right. *I* have no right to force you out. Vid, take the post down. Issue a public apology or something and say you made a mistake. I'll make it easy for you, Jacen. You don't have to choose between me and your future. Let me make that choice for you."

I grab Vidya's hand and lead her out of the cafe. I don't look back.

Tears are clouding my vision, but I let them flow unabated. Breathing hurts. Each heartbeat is painful. I let the pain take over.

Jacen doesn't stop me or chase me. And I don't want him to.

17

I always joked about how lame the scene in the second Twilight movie was, where Bella just sat there looking out the window while the seasons changed. Now I realize how real that scene feels. Vidya took down her post and wrote an apology on her I-G story, but it doesn't really matter now that I've broken things off with Jacen. Why is heartbreak this painful?

Having all universities postpone their semester registration because of the pandemic makes things worse. With nothing to distract me with, I bury myself in battle royale games on my console. Even then, making headshots doesn't give any satisfaction like it used to. I log in and prepare for a matchmaking session, but another player pings me and requests to party up. Elayne. I should shoot at her, not team up with her to shoot others. I ignore her, but she sends a whisper to pester me until I accept her party request. We say nothing while waiting in the lobby, or during the game other than to warn each other about hidden enemies and bonus gear. And she's seriously good. Our party finishes at the top for three consecutive games.

Once we're done for the day, Elayne requests to chat on a private channel. I patch her through after a moment's hesitation.

"Good team effort, Azraai," she says.

"Thanks. You should go professional," I say.

"That's what my brother keeps telling me. See how it goes. If my college is shut down permanently, maybe I'll give it a serious thought."

"It can't be that bad, can it?" I ask, despite myself.

"I don't know. Hey Azraai, can we meet up? Just the two of us?" she asks.

"Why?"

"I feel like I need to clear the air. It's about Jacen."

When has it ever *not* been about Jacen? "There's nothing to talk about."

"Please?"

I sigh and stare at my character on the screen. He looks battered, just like how I feel. I give a long sigh. "Not like I have anything else to do, anyway. Where and what time?"

I regret my decision throughout the drive to KLCC, but it's too late to turn back, partly because the traffic is so heavy both ways, it's not worth making a U-turn without stopping by the mall first. Finding a parking spot is another matter. People are acting as if the lightened MCO means things are back to normal. Watching young couples pushing strollers and carrying toddlers is making me anxious. I adjust my mask to make sure it's snug.

I meet Elayne at the center court, which is uncharacteristically empty. They should put up brightly colored Deepavali decorations by now. I'm not sure if they will lift the interstate travel ban in time for the celebration, but abandoning the decorations altogether feels like giving up on hope. Not that I have anything much to hope for, anyway.

I have difficulty distinguishing Elayne from the crowd, but I guess she doesn't have the same problem. She walks up to me and gives me a small wave. She's wearing a black bucket hat and a blue surgical mask, and an oversized T-shirt that she tucks under her ankle-length jeans. No wonder she didn't need as much time as Vidya usually does to get ready.

"Did you wait long?" she asks over the din of the crowd.

"Just arrived. You?"

"Same. Do you want to get anything to eat?" she asks.

"Not hungry."

Elayne then leads me to a tea stand and orders a cup of bubble milk tea for herself while I order an iced oolong tea with no sugar. She insists on paying for the drinks, so I let her. When she asks me if we can go somewhere quiet to drink and talk, I suggest we take a stroll at the park, even though it's only 4:30 in the afternoon, and it's bound to be scorching hot outside.

Turns out, I'm not that far off. The sun is glaring, but it's also windy. Clouds drift by and occasionally block the sun, making the walk along the jogging track a pleasant one. I stop in the middle of the bridge over the artificial lake and snap a panoramic shot of the twin towers. The fountains dance, one spout towering over the rest, but I'm not sure if they still hold the nightly musical fountain event. Elayne walks to an empty gazebo that offers shade from the sun, and I take a seat across from her. It's nice out here, with just the sounds of the fountain spouts and rustling leaves, and no hint of the horrible traffic all around us.

"So, what do you want to talk about?" I ask. I take a sip from the cup. The tea is slightly bitter. It's good. I take another sip.

Elayne turns the cup in a counter-clockwise manner. "Straight to the point. That's good," she mumbles. She lowers her mask and takes a sip from the big straw.

"I know you went to his house. His parents seemed to like you," I say.

"Did they? That's good. His brother... not so much. He's a little weird."

I balk at this. A small part of me regrets not recording this so that I can send the sound clip to Jacen and let him deal with it. I admit, I can be vindictive. "You know about his brother, right?" I ask. She keeps using Jacen's jacket. Surely she must know its story.

Elayne shrugs. "Jacen doesn't talk about his family much. That's why I went to his home. I wanted to know why he ghosted me after we kissed. We kissed, you know. On the lips. Back at Vidya's party."

I nod. That kiss is something I remember. I feel like telling Elayne about *my* kisses with Jacen, but I stop myself. "So... he ghosted you? Did you guys break up?"

"I broke up with him at the party, but when I returned his jacket, he acted as if nothing happened. After you were hospitalized, he just, I don't know, drifted away," she says.

So Jacen was *not* still keeping her as a backup plan. My heart surges for an instant, but I quell it just as quickly. This changes nothing.

"I was so confused why he treated me that way, but then I saw this," she says. She shows me a screenshot on her phone. Vidya's I-G post. "You guys are dating, aren't you?"

I give a slow nod. I don't see the point of lying. But I feel the need to correct her. "Were," I whisper.

"But it's unnatural. It's against all teachings. It's against *your* teachings. How can two guys be together? It's unnatural," she says without looking at me.

"You fall in love with the person, not the gender," I say.

There it is. I finally admit it to myself. I've fallen in love with Jacen. I love him. But it's too late.

Shaking her head, Elayne says, "It's still wrong. God created people as pairs. Man and woman. Anything else deviates from the natural order."

I sigh and give a small laugh. "A very wise woman told me God *never* makes mistakes. Are you telling me He made a mistake when I was born? When Jacen was born?"

"God sent you his way to tempt him. To test him."

I rise to my feet. The makeup artist Sis's bearded face fills my mind. "Are you listening to yourself, Elayne? What about the people who get Covid? What about all the people who die from it? They don't even get a proper burial. Is this also a test? Will you tell that to the families of those who are struggling for their lives while we sit here debating about *your* concept of what's natural and not?"

Elayne backs slightly away and looks around, likely looking for ways to escape from a crazy queer. But she stands her ground, defiant. I'll give her that. "But you will never give him happiness, Azraai. What about ten years from now, and all his friends have children running about? Can *you* give that to him? A family? A life?"

I clap my hands slowly, deliberately. "Wow. Low blow, Elayne. Well done. Are you telling me you can give him all those things?"

"Between you and me, who do you think his family will choose? Who do you think society will allow?"

Fuck. Checkmate. Fuck.

"Even if Jacen chooses you, he'll be giving up his future. Do you want that, Azraai? Are you that selfish?"

Is there such a thing as *double* checkmate? Fuck me.

Elayne stands in front of me. She needs to crane her neck to look me in the eye, but I'm the one who ends up backing away. "Do the right thing, Azraai. Let him go."

"I have, Elayne."

"He hasn't."

Just my luck. I leave Elayne at the gazebo, but end up bumping into the asshole as I make my way back along the lake. KL can't be *this* small, can it? He falls on his butt and I immediately ball my fist and prepare for a fight, but he seems distracted.

"Sorry," he says, but when he looks up, his face visibly pales.

"What?" I say.

"Azraai. You. I tried contacting you, but you never replied to my

DMs."

"I never read comments and DMs," I absently say.
"So you didn't get my messages?"
I narrow my eyes. "What messages?"
"I need your help."
Well, that's unexpected.

18

We sit at the clinic waiting for our turn to be called. The inside is a stark contrast against bustling Pudu just outside the front doors. The nurse at the registration counter stifles her yawn, but she must have forgotten she's wearing a clear plastic face shield, because she ends up pressing it against her face.

I've seen all kinds of people whenever I visit this clinic, from businessmen in expensive shirts to tired transvestites with uneven breasts. Their walks of life may be vastly different, but their faces show the same expressions while they wait for their blood results. The same face the asshole in front of me is wearing.

He shakes his legs and taps his feet on the floor, sending the metal frame of his chair creaking rhythmically. He keeps biting his nails as he looks at the black overhead screen.

I sit back and close my eyes, but the non-stop creaking is getting on my nerves. "Chill, will you?"

He shoots a glare at me before softening the look. "How can you be so calm?"

"Unlike you, I get tested regularly. And I practice safe sex."

"That's so gay," he mutters.

I sit up and lean forward. "The faster you see the closet you've holed yourself in, the faster you'll accept yourself and get out of it," I say. "And the safer you'll be to others."

He clamps his mouth shut and looks away. After three more times glancing at the screen, he asks, "How much longer?"

"We can go out for a drink first. There's a decent mamak restaurant two doors away."

"I might throw up if I eat," he says.

"Then we wait. Just... stop fidgeting, will you? The noise is annoying."

My number comes up first. I look at the asshole before rising from my seat. "Wait here, okay? There are usually two to three consultation rooms running, so your number should come up soon. Whatever happens... don't do anything stupid. I'll wait for you out here," I say.

He nods. He looks like a boy who's just terrified. All that fight has abandoned him.

I knock on the door and then enter. I'm familiar with the doctor in the consultation room. He looks young, but I overheard a nurse once telling her colleague about celebrating his 52nd birthday. He has kind eyes. I like looking at his eyes when he gives his consultation.

The doctor looks up from his computer and raises an eyebrow. "*You're* patient 0025? It hasn't been six months since your last visit, has it? Anything interesting happened?"

There's no point in bringing up anonymity when you visit the same clinic for regular tests. I give a heavy sigh and sit across from the doctor. He's wearing a surgical mask and a face shield, but his eyes are clearly visible. That's good.

"So you want to go straight to your result or do you want to talk about it for a bit?" he asks.

"Well, there's this asshole—"

"That's not nice," he says.

"Wait till you hear the story," I say.

Still chuckling, the doctor waves his hand for me to continue talking.

"This asshole kept bugging me in uni and called me a faggot. I didn't care about that, but he was just in my face, so I took things into my own hands. Literally." I smile at the thought. Jacen would appreciate the pun. I sigh again.

"Then what happened?"

"I gave him a blowjob, and he came in my mouth."

"That's risky," the doctor says.

"Tell him that. He held my head and stopped me from letting go of his dick. Good thing I didn't swallow any of it."

"That's dangerous of him."

"It gets better. Someone recorded us, and he panicked and brought his friends to beat me to a pulp. Wait. How come I didn't think of this?

The ringtone. Fuck me," I say.

"I get why you called him that. So now where is he?"

I point at the door with the back of my thumb. "Waiting for his turn to be called. Apparently, he went out cruising a few days before the blowjob and the guy turned out to be positive."

"Covid or HIV?"

I chuckle. "Good one, doc. You know which one. So the asshole is panicking outside."

The doctor leans forward and studies my face. "And you brought him here to get tested?"

"I remember my first time here. It's not something anyone should go through alone," I say.

"You're a good man, you know that? A kind soul. We need more people like you."

There's a tinge of bitterness in my laughter. "People like me will go straight to hell, doc."

Without looking away or changing his expression, he says, "Won't we all? It's how you spend your time here that matters. Now, are you ready for your result?"

"Hit me."

The doctor chuckles. "Well, patient 0025. Your result is non-reactive. Congratulations. Make sure you keep practicing safe sex, you hear?"

"Thanks, doc. Sure thing."

He points at the round fishbowl filled with colorful packets of condoms on his desk. "Take a few packets and get out of here."

While he is being consulted in another room, I wait for the asshole in the common area. I take out my phone and open I-G. I browse through my feed, not particularly interested in any of the photos, so I type in Jacen's user name. His last post was over two weeks ago. It's the selfie I took outside the hawker center. Both of us looked so happy, so carefree. He didn't put a caption, just the lightly edited photo, and the post received 11 likes out of his 57 followers. He must not have approved all the new follow requests except for Vidya's. Jacen sure likes his privacy.

I give another sigh and replay my conversation with Elayne. She's right. I'll just bring him misery and potential scares like this one. He won't have a life with me. I click on his profile and then on the three dots at the top right corner. I take a long look at my screen before tapping the word 'block' written in red letters. This will make it easier for him to let me go.

I know the asshole's result before he tells it to me because the relief is obvious when he steps out of the consultation room. "I'm negative," he says.

"Me, too."

He releases an audible sigh that holds the weight of his anxiety. "Thank you. That was scary. Thank you for bringing me here. For waiting for me." He offers his hand, which I don't take. "By the way, my name is—"

"I don't want to know your name. Ever. I don't want to be your friend. I just want to know one thing," I say.

He looks taken aback. He blinks stupidly and retracts his hand. "What do you want to know?"

"The guy who recorded us. He's your friend, isn't he? I heard the same ringtone after you guys beat me up."

The asshole looks at his shoes and starts fidgeting again.

"Was it a setup?"

He immediately looks at me, his eyes wide. "No. I knew you liked to use that toilet, so I tried my luck a few times to run into you there."

"You could have just asked for it nicely," I say.

"I'm not a fag... sorry. But when my friend showed me the clip, I panicked. I figured if I took the lead, no one would suspect me."

I fight the urge to punch him in the face. "I don't care what you do with your life, but don't endanger someone else again. And get tested regularly."

"Can we get tested together again?"

"What part of 'I don't want to be your friend' don't you understand? This is a one-off thing."

Now that the asshole has gotten his result and counseling, I don't see any reason to hang out any longer. I take my things and leave him standing at the clinic.

I store the test result and the free packets of condoms in my underwear locker. It's been a long day, and dealing with two of my least favorite people in the span of hours has taken years out of my life. What I feel is old, spent. I collapse on my bed and welcome sleep, but it refuses to come. I flip over, sit up, and reach for the Epiphone. My skin is healing after I haven't played a song in a while. Rubbing the calluses between my thumb and middle finger reminds me of Jacen. Sitting at the edge of the bed playing the guitar reminds me of Jacen.

Fuck. *Everything* reminds me of Jacen.

I look at my I-G profile. I've snapped an entire gallery's worth of Jacen's candid photos, but I posted none of them. Not even one. I told myself it was out of respect for his privacy, but what if Jacen was right? What if I am a hypocrite?

A soft knock on the door pulls me back to reality. I wipe my eyes. I didn't know they were wet. "Is it time for dinner, Mak Su?" I ask.

"It's me," says the old man. He hangs out in the open doorway, waiting for an invitation.

I sit straighter and return the Epiphone to its stand. I grab a used T-shirt from the carpet and use it to quickly rub my eyes before rolling it into a ball and throwing it in the laundry hamper. "Why are you here? Anything happened?" I ask. All three least favorite people in the world in one day. I must have screwed up my karma big time.

The old man gives a soft laugh and points at my gaming chair. "May I?"

I shrug and watch as he sits on the leather chair and leans back as far as the seat allows.

"This is a good chair. Maybe I should get one for my office. And the library," he says.

With the old man, it's all about who blinks first. I sit on the bed and keep quiet. He sits on the chair and keeps quiet. I have no issues out-silencing him, but I have to take a shit soon.

The old man clears his throat. Thank God, because I don't know if I can hold on for long. "Are you doing okay?" he asks.

"You already asked me that."

"Suzita said you and Jacen haven't been hanging out together. Did something happen?"

Mental note: tell Mak Su not to discuss my life with the old man.

"We were friends. Now we're not. This kind of thing happens."

"But he was more than just a friend," he says.

I study his face. He doesn't avert his gaze. "You *know* about me?"

"I've always known, son. I don't know if Suzita—"

"Oh, she knows," I cut him off.

"There you go. All three of your parents have always known," he says.

"Three?"

"Your mother. She was the first to know, and she loved you all the more for it. She protected you with everything she had. And she called you—"

"Her perfect son."

The old man nods. "I don't know if you remember this, but kids in Primary School used to tease you and bully you for preferring to play with the girls instead of the boys. And you loved getting makeup on for your kindergarten concerts."

"Now I endorse makeup lines. Go figure," I say.

That earns me another chuckle. "Son, what do you remember about the accident?"

Well, this trip down memory lane sure veers south real quick. "Nothing much. Just that Mama protected me from slipping out of the seatbelt and she died on the spot. I still can't see her face."

The old man nods. "And it's *my* fault."

Wait. I grew up assuming he blamed *me* for the accident. "What do you mean, it's your fault?"

The old man swivels his chair sideways and stares out the window. "I had always been scared for your future. What if the world turned against you, beat you down, just for being you? I wanted to change you, not because I didn't love who you were, but I was desperate for the world to love you back. We would fight, your mother and I. And you would hide in Suzita's room whenever we fought. On the day of the accident, you came back from school all beaten up, but you refused to tell us who did that to you. I guess some things never change."

"Maybe I was mugged then, too," I say dryly.

"I guess we'll never know. When you came back from school all bruised up, we got into a big fight. I may have used some unsavory names to describe you because I was terrified. But your mother told me I used those words because I hated you, that I couldn't accept you for the perfect boy you were." He lets out a long sigh. "Deep down, I knew she was right. You're my only son, and who will carry on our family legacy when you're gone? Who will take care of you when I'm gone?"

"Pa, it's not your fault. It was an accident."

The old man stares at me and blinks. His eyes start to pool. "You haven't called me that in years," he says.

I blink in return. I didn't realize I called him that.

"It's my fault we got into a fight that day. I should have stopped her from driving you away. It's my fault I didn't get into the car or follow you. It's my fault your mother was taken away from you so soon."

"She was taken from you, too," I whisper.

"And it's my fault you can't see her face. Your therapist told me the damage was related to something much deeper. I am that reason. You have her face. Her nose, her lips, her eyes. Even her hair. You have my business acumen, my beard, and my family's height, but that's it. And looking at you after I lost her... it was too much for me. Every day you look more and more like her, especially when you shave. Seeing you walking around the house is like seeing her ghost."

"Do I really look like her?"

"You even have her soft freckles."

We sit quietly for a while, but it's no longer oppressive. For the first time in years, I can breathe when he's in the same room. And I don't feel like running away. "Pa, Dato' Hanis said something about you using your influence on her. What did she mean by that?" I finally say.

He raises an eyebrow. "She did? She promised never to reveal my involvement in your career."

"What do you mean, involvement?"

"Son, the world can be a terrible place. I just do all I can to shelter you for as long as possible."

"But you never told me anything."

He reaches over but changes his mind. He leans back in the chair. "Sometimes love is not meant to be seen. It's enough that I get to see you flourish and live your best life."

"Did you make the clip disappear?" I ask.

"You should thank my assistant for that. He's an IT whizz."

"Is he in that WhatsApp group?"

"I told him to vote for #QanAz. Sounds like panas. Everyone loves a hot romance," he says with a straight face.

I hide my face in my hands. "That's so wrong, Pa." Then, I look up at him and say, "Dato' Hanis threatened Vidya's career if I made a fuss."

"She did? I'll have a word with her. But you should have more faith in your friend. Her parents told me about all the international endorsements she's getting on her Instagram. You youngsters have the world at the tip of your fingers," Papa says.

"Literally," I say.

"Did she tell you that a French modeling agency wants to sign her up once this pandemic is over and commercial flights can resume as usual again?" Papa asks.

I shake my head. "No. She did not mention that."

"Hanis cannot control *that* kind of career, now, can she?"

"No, she cannot," I say. "Pa, Jacen said I'm sheltered and privileged, and he doesn't have the same luxury. He's right, isn't he?"

Papa strokes his beard as he contemplates an answer. "He's right, but that doesn't make your life any easier than his. You'll face different challenges and adversaries. Just being you, having accepted who you are from a young age, takes absolute bravery. Bravery that I can only pray for."

"He also called me a hypocrite."

"I don't have an answer to that. Only you have the right to your own truth. I'm only here as your safety net. Who knows, maybe one day you and Jacen will be each other's safety net. If not him, then someone else. But I like Jacen. I can tell that he loves you so much. Maybe as much as I loved your mother," Papa says.

"Maybe in another life, Pa. Besides, I blocked him on I-G and Facebook. There's no way he saw the video."

"Don't be too sure about that."

"What do you mean by that?"

Instead of answering, Papa slaps his thighs and stands up. "I'm serious about the chair. Maybe I'll get my assistant to buy this for the entire office. Thank you for not shutting me out, son."

My eyes start to pool again, and I use the blanket to dry them. "Thank you for being there for me, Pa."

Papa stops at the doorway and turns back to look at me. "I love you, son. And I'm proud of you. Always own your truth."

19

Yesterday I announced on I-G and Facebook that I'll be doing a live stream tonight at ten. I've set up my room into a mini studio, with three mic stands: two for the Epiphone and one for me to sing into. I've rehearsed the entire day to make sure everything comes out perfectly.

I start the live stream ten minutes early to allow the crowd to build up. It's weird that I've done live shows in front of big crowds before, but my palms never sweated as they do now. By ten, I've accumulated over six thousand viewers on both platforms. That's way more than I expected. I let them greet one another, and many positive emojis flood the screen.

I take the Epiphone and check the tuning one last time. Looking at the screen, I say nothing. I just start singing Calum Scott's version of Robyn's "Dancing on My Own".

I let the last F note trail off before putting the Epiphone away. The comments sections are filled with heart emojis and song requests. When the viewer count exceeds fifty thousand concurrent viewers, I blink multiple times. I definitely *did not* expect this viewership. I try not to let the comments distract me.

"Hi, guys. Thanks for tuning in. The song wasn't my announcement, but it was just as important. I had an interesting conversation with my dad yesterday. Yes, Vid. My dad. He told me about owning my truth.

"I told someone very important to me I wanted to love in the light, and not hide in darkness. I've always been honest about who I am, but that honesty is not complete. All I wanted was for that person to love me openly, but I haven't done that for myself.

"We live in a society where being different is frowned upon. It's not encouraged. Worse, it's not talked about. If you don't have a conversation about it, the issue doesn't exist.

"And it's unhealthy, this norm that we've always embraced. We're living a new norm now. So maybe it's time for a change. More than once, I've been told that I can embrace who I am because I am privileged. And they are right. I have my family to lift me. I have a beautiful, crazy, annoying friend to lift me. But a lot of others don't have the same loving environment that I have.

"I've been beaten up a few times because of who I am. I lost my parents because of who I am. But lucky for me, I got one parent back. And he's the one who encouraged me to share my truth. To own it.

"Truth is, I am gay. I like guys. I've always liked guys. And I am so sorry if I've misled anyone. I am sorry to my #AzraAiNi fan club. Yes, I know about you guys and I appreciate your support and attention.

"Who I am, what I am, is not a phase that I'll soon grow out of. It's part of who I am, part of my identity. It's not a disease, and it's not contagious. You don't turn gay if you befriend one. Even if you do, there's no shame in that. I've never been ashamed of who I am, but there are people out there who take pleasure in reminding me that my existence is wrong. My existence is *not* wrong. And if you're watching this, *your* existence is not wrong. Whichever God you pray to or not created you just the way you're meant to. *I see you.* And I hope you'll see one another.

"I'm sure I've just made my life that much harder by sharing this with the world. And I'm not saying that you should come out, whoever you are. If you're comfortable staying hidden, there's no shame in that. *I see you.* If you plan to come out and you need someone to talk to, hit me up. *I see you.* I may take some time to answer because I don't really read my DMs, but we'll find a way to make it work.

"For those of you who are still listening in, thank you. I feel loved. I feel privileged to be seen. And I see you, too. And I love you."

20

In movies, a montage with uplifting music that leads to a happy ending follows such an announcement. But this is *not* a movie.

Dato' Hanis was right. Actions have consequences. Even during my announcement last week, the heart emojis and positive comments were replaced by angry and poop emojis and name-calling. My viewership dropped so much that when I ended the video, only 956 still tuned in.

And it didn't stop there. My followers on I-G and subscribers on Facebook dropped by over 100,000 that night alone, and the count is still dropping. I would have been in so much trouble if I had engaged with endorsements and sponsorship deals. But they're not satisfied with unfollowing me. People are leaving comments on my posts from four years ago, telling me to repent and to return to the right path. I get links to videos on conversion and treatment for homosexuality. I get advice on how to treat my 'condition'.

Dato' Hanis has made it clear that she'll never hire me or Vidya ever again. Even our agent announced two days ago that he's not renewing our contract. The university is, however, surprisingly chill about it. I had a meeting with the Dean earlier today, and he told me that whatever I did in my personal time was up to me, but my extracurricular activities should be kept *outside* campus borders. Of course, it helped that Papa was sitting beside me the whole time. Business 101: capitalize on every advantage that you have. Or maybe that's from *Art of War*.

What I find annoying, however, is that whenever I get a notification from I-G or Facebook, it's bound to be some death threat or unsolicited advice. Sometimes both. And the notifications keep flooding in.

"Jesus Christ, babe. Turn off notifications. I'm trying to enjoy this heavenly cup of coffee here," Vidya says as she sips from her cup. Of course, she has taken a picture of the latte art in both our cups before allowing me to touch mine.

"Vid, I'm really, really sorry," I say from across the small round table.

"It's not my loss if people here don't want me to grace their designs and spreads. Stop apologizing already. It doesn't suit you," Vidya says with a nonchalant face.

"But it's my fault."

Vidya rolls her eyes. Exactly the reaction I'm fishing for. "For Christ's sake, babe, enough already. It's not your fault that the designer is a vindictive hag. Wait till I find out the amount of Botox and implants she has on and release the statement."

"Vid."

She holds her hands up. "Kidding. Maybe. But you should have come out for me too during your sexy monologue."

"Who are you gonna cheat off, then? Girls are way more competitive than guys," I say with a shudder."

"Fair point. You know, I wanted to tap you right then. You were so sexy. 'I see you'. I still get goosebumps."

"Seriously?"

"No. Who do you think I am? One of your fans? Rohan can't stop talking about it, though. Sure you don't want to get on with him? You have my blessing," Vidya says.

I clear my throat. "Speaking of, how's the group?"

Vidya stares at the screen and scrolls using her perfectly manicured forefinger. "Quiet. Many people left. They feel betrayed. I guess the QuanAz hashtag got too real."

"There's no #QuanAz, Vid. See, I'm dancing on my own."

Vidya reaches over and holds my hand. "Babe, *I'm* your dance partner. Don't forget that."

Just as we're about to leave, Vidya's phone dings. She looks at the screen, stands up, and then sits back down. Her eyes are the widest I've ever seen yet. I sit back down, ready to catch her if she develops an aneurysm or something.

"Babe. Have you seen your Insta?"

I check my account. Nothing out of the ordinary other than more unsolicited sage advice. I guess this is *my* new norm, then. I look at

Vidya, confused.

"Your feed. Quan's account."

"I blocked him," I say.

Vidya balls her fist and bites her lower lip. "You... Jesus fucking Christ, Azraai. Of all the times for me to go on an Insta cleanse.... Why did you block him?"

"Why?"

"Hold on. Let me log into my account. Ah. Holy mother of..."

Vidya hands me her phone. The screen shows Jacen's I-G profile, but he posted a grid of nine photos that make up a black-and-white picture of two hands intertwined. Our hands in my car. When I scroll up, the grid of nine photos makes up a picture of...

"You, babe. He posted your face," Vidya says. She's gushing and jumping in her seat. "This Quan has some serious talent."

The third grid series is of me walking forward, looking back. Behind my head is the sun, its rays creating a halo effect around me. I forget to breathe when I read the caption on each of the nine photos.

zhenxinquan2001 I want to love in the light. You are my light.

"Who told you about this?" I ask Vidya.

"They showed screenshots of Quan's Insta profile in your WhatsApp fan group."

"It's still alive? But Jacen's profile is private," I say.

"Not anymore. It's public. And he's raking up followers. They have revived the hashtag. Babe, they have revived the hashtag!"

Ever since I saw Jacen's photo of me, I've learned to love sunny days. But I still love rainy days the best. When I walk into my usual joint, June the barista tells me that Jacen has transferred back to his old outlet over a month ago, around the time after we broke up.

I have to keep reminding myself that he never called me his boyfriend.

By the time I leave the building, a deluge has formed outside. KL and its flash storms. I can either get another drink and wait inside, or I can run to my car and get drenched. Absolute no-brainer. I take one tentative step, then two, and then run toward my car. It feels good, running in the rain. I breathe through my mouth, and I huff out all the water that slips in when I exhale. Rainwater drips from my lashes, breaking my vision into a kaleidoscope of car lights bokeh. My hair is plastered on my scalp, and my turtleneck top clings to my body. So do my jeans. The rain soaks right into my shorties. My shoes slosh as I run, and I don't care that I stomp on puddles on the street. A cold wind whips at me, and my whole body shivers involuntarily, up to the roots of my hair. There's something about running in the rain that makes me feel alive.

Someone is standing in the rain beside my car. Someone tall. I slow down, and my steps turn tentative. He's shivering, just as I'm shivering. Two idiots standing in the pouring rain.

"Jacen?" I ask even though I know it's him.

"Oh, thank God. I thought I was going to stand here until the rain stopped," he says. His teeth are chattering.

"What are you doing here?" I ask over the roar of the rain and wind.

"What does it look like? Can we get in the car already?" he shouts back.

I unlock the car and jump in, and so does Jacen. Pools are already forming in our seats, and condensation fogs the inner windscreen. Wiping my hand on my drenched jeans, I start the engine and crank up the air-conditioning to 26C. I look at Jacen. Both of us are shivering uncontrollably.

"How long were you waiting for me?" I ask.

"June told me when you came, and I asked one of my friends to cover the rest of my shift. I thought you were never coming to that outlet again."

"You could have just called me," I say.

Grinning, he says, "But this gesture is grander."

Well, he got me there.

"You blocked me on Instagram and Facebook? No wonder I couldn't tag you. I waited for some response, but when you kept quiet, I thought I was too late," he says. Even with his teeth chattering, I can catch the accusation in his voice.

"Let's get out of these wet clothes first. I don't want to get sick."

"Sure, but not your place. I don't want to disturb Mak Su," he says.

"And my dad," I say.

"Not 'old man' anymore?"

I flash him a half-grin. "When you said you didn't want to disturb Mak Su, did you mean…"

"Just get us out of here," Jacen says. He mirrors my grin.

For the record, getting a hard-on under drenched shorties and jeans is *not* a comfortable feeling.

We check in at a container hotel near Bukit Bintang. I had in mind a fancy five-star hotel with an enormous bathtub that can fit two tall guys, but since Jacen insisted on paying, I drove us here instead. The room at the end of the row is small, just enough for a queen-sized bed on the elevated floor next to a wall-panel window, a rack beside the entrance, and a cramped bathroom I need to almost squeeze in to enter. I slide the key into its slot to turn on the electricity and reach inside the bathroom for the two towels rolled on a shelf under the sink. I hand one to Jacen.

"You take the shower first. You stood in the rain longer than I did," I say.

Jacen towel-dries his hair and shakes his head. "No, you go ahead. I'm just damp. You're still drenched."

I won't argue with that. I enter the bathroom, slide the door closed, and strip peel off my clothes. Each article lands on the cool tiled floor with a heavy thump. I let the hot shower warm me up nicely. Just as I'm about to pump the soap dispenser, the door slides open and Jacen steps in, the towel wrapped around his waist. His wet muscles ripple with each movement.

"What are you doing?" I ask.

Jacen drops the towel on the floor. "Something I should have done long ago," he says.

The shower booth is a snug fit for one person, but two tall, athletic guys trying to squeeze in are almost comical. We end up dumping the wet clothes in the shower stall, unhooking the showerhead, and taking turns showering each other in front of the toilet bowl.

"Not the romantic scene I had in mind," Jacen says.

I sputter a laugh. "I wanted to bring us to a place where we could both fit into the tub, let alone the entire bathroom."

"Next time," he says. It sounds like a promise.

Things get interesting when there's soap involved. I take several pumps and lather the liquid on Jacen's shoulders and back. He tenses when I slide my hands across the landscape of his body. I can feel the power underneath his smooth skin. I sit on the toilet bowl and reach down to lather his small but perfect butt cheeks, and then his legs. He gasps sharply when I slide up his inner thigh. I turn him around. He is throbbing hard.

"Azraai..." he breathes.

I point the shower head at his shaft, clean my hands, and then start stroking him. How much it will hurt is something I can already imagine. I stroke him until his head is freed from its foreskin. His breaths get sharper when I touch the sensitive head. He whimpers when I take him in my mouth. I release him when his body bunches up, and let him catch his breath.

"My turn," Jacen says after a few deep breaths. He pumps a generous amount of shampoo on his hands and attends to my hair.

"Seriously, Jace?" I ask, wiping suds from my eyes.

"Just wait," he says and massages my scalp. He applies pressure on his fingertips and then lifts them immediately. He repeats the movement throughout my scalp. My eyes roll upward from the pleasure the sensation brings. He then pumps soap in his hands and traces his smooth fingers on my face, applying just enough pressure for me to feel it. I close my eyes.

Jacen kneels on the floor and steals a quick kiss. When I open my eyes, he's grinning. I lean forward for another kiss, but he stops me and continues lathering my neck and shoulders. He massages my arms one by one and then gives his full attention to my chest and abs.

"Damn, Azraai. You're big," he says. His eyes look worried.

"That's what everyone says," I say with a smirk.

"Don't spoil the mood."

"Okay, okay. Sorry."

Instead of giving me the same service I gave him, Jacen washes my thighs and legs and only gives my painfully throbbing dick a once-over before turning off the shower. When I question him with a look, he just takes my towel and pats me dry, and then dries himself. His movements are careful, gentle. Before I can entertain my disappointment, he grabs my shaft and leads me to the bed. He pushes me down, just like I did in my room, and then crouches over me. He is unbelievably hard, and so am I. He lowers himself and kisses me. Gentle at first, but we get hungry fast. He bites my lower lip and pulls it, and then pushes his tongue into my mouth. He tastes like mint. Did he prepare himself for this encounter? He then kisses my jaw, my Adam's apple, my chest, my nipples, and all the way down until he wraps me in his mouth. His motions are sloppy and awkward, so I hold his head to guide him. When he finally releases me, he takes a deep breath before flicking his tongue around my butthole.

I take a sharp intake of breath. "Fuck, that's new."

Jacen looks up and half-grins. "So how are we gonna do this?" he asks.

"I have a condom in my wallet."

He bounds for the bathroom and returns with a wet, squished box and a tube of lube.

"You came prepared, didn't you?" I ask, seriously impressed.

"Who's going to..." he asks, staring at my dick.

"Come here," I say.

I open the box, tear a foil package, and roll the condom over his dick. I then apply a generous amount of lube and stroke his shaft a few times. I lie down on the bed with a pillow under my butt and pull him close with my legs. "I don't really like to bottom, so if we're gonna have more of these encounters, we have to discuss logistics," I say.

Jacen widens his eyes in horror, but the look quickly changes as I guide him inside me. After the initial excruciating pain and the weird, full sensation in my bowel that makes me feel like I need to take a shit immediately, the sensations settle down to something almost bearable. He goes slow at first, but when I encourage him to go faster, he complies.

Jacen explodes inside me, and once he's spent, he lies on top of me. His body spasms with each pulse of release. He slips the condom off his semi-hard dick and then looks at me with a serious glint in his eyes. "Your turn," he says.

"My turn for what?"

Jacen takes a foil packet and tears it with his mouth. He rolls the slick rubber on my shaft.

"Jace, we don't have to do this."

"I know," he says as he lubes me up.

Jacen lies facedown on the bed and spreads his legs. I lube up his butt and introduce a finger. He yelps in pain and pulls away. Once he settles down, I try again. He bites a pillow and yowls into it, but he refuses to let me stop. Eventually, I get him to relax enough to slide my dick in, ever so slowly. He yowls again, but when I withdraw, he flails and somehow grabs my butt cheeks and pulls me closer. It takes a few tries before he's comfortable with the rhythm. He pushes me out, turns over, and signals me to continue. He's hard again.

I pull out when I'm about to explode, but he locks me with his legs. Once spent, I shudder and collapse on the bed beside him. We're both drenched in sweat and will need to shower again, but I don't have any energy left to even reach for the used condom.

Jacen pulls me toward him and uses his arm as my pillow. He plays with my hair and draws circles on my shoulder. We stay like this as the rain pitter-patters on the window.

"You think anyone heard us?" he asks.

"I think the entire world heard you," I say.

Jacen chuckles as he hugs me closer. "I'm going to be sore for a few days, aren't I?"

"Probably. Hey, Jace?"

"Hmm?" His chest rumbles against the side of my head when he hums.

"What made you change your mind? You've thrown away your future for this. For me."

"Someone shared your coming out video. What you did was brave, and I wanted to be brave, too. Besides, who said anything about throwing away my future? I'm going to fight for it like I always have. Things are just more... challenging. And I like a good challenge."

I can't help but chuckle. "I bet I know who shared that video. But what about your family?" I ask.

"Zhe Jie was the one who kept reminding me I liked you."

"Your parents?"

Jacen shrugs. His face turns distant, a little sad. "They'll come around. Eventually. We're a practical family. I'm paying for my siblings' education, so it makes little sense to kick me out. Don't worry about it, okay? You know what, I'm so glad I hit you with the football."

I sit up and look at him, wide-eyed. "Wait. That was intentional?"

Jacen smiles, washing away all that sadness. "I wanted to approach you since orientation week, but I didn't know how. We were in different groups, and you were *always* with Vidya."

Chuckling, I say. "The power couple of the campus. If only they knew."

"And when you put on makeup for me during the photo shoot, I was so hard, I was afraid to get out of the chair."

"You too? It wasn't just me, then. What about the free meal? Was that part of your plan to go out with me?"

"That, and the movie, too. But I thought you were with Vidya, and you encouraged me to go out with Elayne," he says.

"Yeah, that was my bad."

"No, it wasn't. If I didn't go out with her, I wouldn't have admitted to myself that I wanted to be with you. That I wanted *you*. And you're worth everything."

Just like that, I fall for him all over again, this time completely.

"Hey, Azraai?"

"Hmm?"

Jacen turns to his side, props up on his elbow, and studies my face. "Will you be my boyfriend?"

I scrunch my nose. "I'm not into labels."

He playfully punches my knee. "Shut up."

"Jace?"

"Hmm?"

"I love you."

Jacen plants a long kiss on my lips. "I love you more," he says.

When I wake up in the middle of the night, the rain has stopped. Jacen is lightly snoring beside me. I pull the curtain slightly open to let the light in. We're both naked under the blanket, and watching the rise and fall of his chest mesmerizes me. His face is beautiful, symmetrical. I gently push a strand of hair from his eyebrow and watch him sleep. The entire world is quiet. I feel at peace, more than I have in a long time.

When I turn, I see a blurred figure standing at the edge of the bed. Instead of being alarmed, I feel the warmth and comfort emanating from her. She feels familiar, somehow. She is dressed in a familiar simple white dress and a billowing skirt, and her chestnut curls reach her shoulders. Her face is beautiful, kind. Her eyes are light brown with green flecks, and her nose is sharp. The tip is slightly upturned. Her lips have the most perfect cupid's bow, and her bone structure is defined, elegant. It's almost like looking in the mirror.

"Ma," I whisper. A single tear rolls down my cheek. I can finally see her face.

A glow of white light surrounds her, and shafts of bright light illuminate her from behind. The light no longer obscures her face but frames it. Defines it. She smiles at me. I smile back.

She shimmers and gradually fades away with the light until only her gentle, loving face remains.

"I'll be all right, Ma," I whisper. "I am loved, and I see you."

THE END

Made in the USA
Columbia, SC
17 July 2022

63289777R00093